Gary taught for over 33 years in 6 schools, leading three as head teacher. His passion for WW1 began when, with colleagues, he developed educational visits to Ypres. Now a key note speaker and educational trainer, he is co-author of four successful books for teachers. He is married with two grown up children and likes sport, mountaineering, football and cycling. He is passionate about a brilliant education for all.

For the fallen.

# Gary Toward

# THE MAGPIE

AUSTIN MACAULEY PUBLISHERS™

LONDON * CAMBRIDGE * NEW YORK * SHARJAH

A CIP catalogue record for this title is available from the British Library.

ISBN 9781786930088 (Paperback)
ISBN 9781787101715 (E-Book)
www.austinmacauley.com

First Published (2017)
Austin Macauley Publishers Ltd.
25 Canada Square
Canary Wharf
London
E14 5LQ

# Acknowledgements

Rushden and District History Society Research Group
*Into the Silence, The Great War, Mallory and the Conquest of Everest* – Wade Davis
*Britain's Last Tommies* – Richard Van Emden
*Magnificent But Not War: The Second Battle of Ypres 1915* – John Dixon
The Imperial War Museum Podcasts, Voices of the First World War.
Ypres map courtesy of Sozzij Illustrations.

I have been fascinated by the events of what we now call The First World War since a young age. In writing this book, I have attempted to weave a story of fiction into the realities of the time as accurately as possible.

I would like to thank my friends Alan, Chris, Matt and Mark who helped me with research and acted as sounding boards for my ideas. Also, grateful thanks to Poppy and Penny for their creative and sympathetic support with editing.

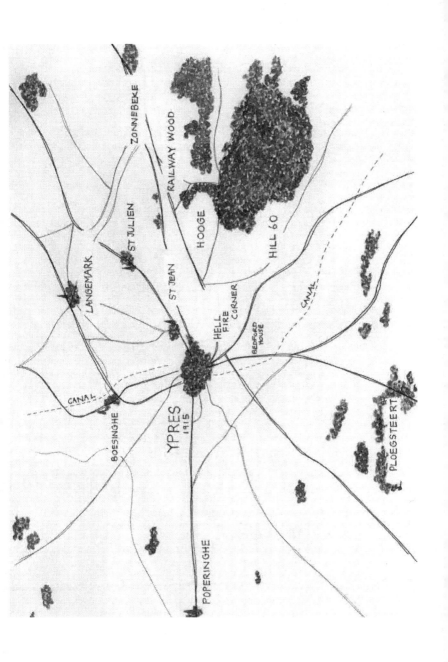

# December, 1913, Durham, England

A cold wind whistled down the banks of the River Wear, rattling at the magnificent stained glass windows of the great cathedral. Possibly the finest example of medieval architecture in Britain, for nine hundred years its towers had been watching over the town, its vast interior offering sanctuary and peace to all around.

John Mitchell looked up at his life's work and glowed with pride. As a stonemason, like his father and grandfather before him, he had toiled almost every day of his adult life to maintain the stonework of St Cuthbert's final resting place. There was not a stone in this vast building he did not know and many of them owed their honourable place in its walls to him. Having packed away his tools, John smiled to himself. His father had given him his first chisel and begun teaching him to carve solid rock at the age of eight. He looked forward to the day when he could do the same for Andrew, his own son, born only two days earlier. The family trade would continue.

Leaving the cathedral behind, John made his way past the castle down onto the cobbled streets of the city before taking a short cut to the river. This was his way home every evening, and tonight in the gloom of the autumn, he knew every twist, turn and cobble. Pausing at the junction with the riverside path, he buttoned his coat against the icy fingers of the north wind. It whistled down the Wear into John's face, nipping at his ears. There was an edge to it that made him think snow was soon to follow and he made a mental note to check the coal shed when he got home. The last thing he wanted was a cold house for his new son. He pulled his thick collar up to protect his ears. Few had ever owned such a coat. Emblazoned on the chest was the crest of Durham City, with a mallet and chisel crossed below: only the cathedral stonemasons ever wore this badge. Each brass button bore the same unique mark. Being formally presented with his coat on the day his apprenticeship was completed was a huge honour for John.

Since that day, as his hands grew rougher, he'd gradually risen through the ranks of the local masons until he finally reached the position of foreman for the whole cathedral. Trusted by the bishop, he now led a team who were gradually replacing the facing stones of the north facade. The weather had taken its toll on the building and while it was possibly the most original of all of the ancient cathedrals in Britain, it still needed constant maintenance. John's project would take ten years to complete. He smiled; by then he would have introduced his son to stonework.

The river was in full flow, well fed by the recent rains that had lashed the moors and farmland to the west. In the dying light he could see a heron, still fishing from a partly submerged fallen tree. It was a beautiful spot, a chocolate box image, even at dusk. This place drew people to the town and would do so for years to come. Taking a last look at his hungry neighbour, John turned and headed for home, back to his wife and his new son.

11

Detective Constable Frank Bolam looked through the swirling mist at the body. It was wedged in the cleft of a large willow branch trapped on the lip of the weir and a pale hand waved, almost gracefully, rocked by the current. Bolam could see little from his position on the riverbank, but from his vantage point he guessed the body was male. The shape of the muscular back and hint of baldness led him in this direction. He would however, have to wait to confirm his thoughts. Unlike the heron he could see precariously perched nearby, there was no way he would wade into the water in this weather. Only a week ago the river's edges were glistening with ice after a week of severely cold weather. He'd wait for his constable to fetch a rowing boat from the rental hut and enlist help from the growing crowd of observers milling around behind him.

This was the third murder case in Bolam's career. Indeed it had been a murder that had prompted his unlikely rise to the rank of detective. A young police constable from a mining family was unusual enough, but one with the imagination and determination to track down the killer of a local baker's wife was unique.

Born the fourth child of five, Frank James Bolam was one of only three who survived past the age of sixteen. His two elder brothers, along with his father and uncle, lost their lives with 160 other men when the Seaham pit exploded. After the news broke, Frank's pregnant mother was one of the hundreds who rushed to the pit head with him and his sister. Waiting for over fourteen painful hours, it eventually became clear to her she'd lost most of her family and she swore her youngest would never venture underground.

The year was 1880 and Frank had been eight months old at the time. As the years passed, he often wondered what it would have been like to have known his father and, in many ways, this thought drove him and influenced the decisions he made, particularly where children were concerned.

On reflection, Bolam thought, finding the so called 'Hot Cross Bun' murderer was easy. At the time though, a piece of luck was needed to help him, but it was that luck that would change his life. The murderer's nickname came about as the victim was found on the bakery floor with a spilled rising dough mix for the Easter fancies beside her. She'd been strangled, her wedding ring taken and the bakery robbed. It was a week later while on duty at Roker Park, as Sunderland played Aston Villa in front of a huge crowd, that Bolam heard a man in the crowd trying to sell a gold wedding band. Playing on a hunch, he took the man in for questioning and it wasn't long before his sergeant had extracted a confession. Bolam's hunch paid off more than he expected. When his station superintendent gained promotion to the City of Durham force, he requested Bolam join him as a detective constable.

The boat arrived after a twenty minute wait and the constable managed to steer it to the water's edge. By this time the crowd had bloated to over twenty and the wind had increased, making the conditions near the weir even more hazardous. Bolam grabbed a strong looking man peering over the edge of the river and gently nudged him into the boat. "There's a pint in it for you if you help me sort this one out, Sam." Bolam smiled at the man. He knew him well and regularly gave him a bed for the night after Sam had taken a few too many glasses of strong ale. With no argument from the conscript, the constable pushed away from the bank with an oar and made for the body.

Just getting near to the edge of the weir without getting into difficulty was a tricky job, but Bolam managed to jam a boathook into the lip of the weir to stabilise their small craft. Sam whipped a length of rope between an oarlock and the tree branch, which allowed him and the constable to roll the body into the boat. Wet through, it took the full strength of both men to gain enough momentum. The body twisted, slowly at first, almost as if it was waking from a strange slumber, onto the edge of the boat before tumbling in on its back.

Lifeless eyes stared at Bolam. He gasped, his knees buckled and he sat back into the boat. He knew this man. He'd known him since he started in Durham and he respected him, not only for his crucial role in the city, but also for his calm manner with his men. Never in his darkest nightmares did Bolam expect to see John Mitchell this way. Only two days ago he'd shared a glass of whisky with the mason to celebrate his lad's birth. Another boy who would never know his father. Bolam steeled himself, there was work to be done, and he nodded at Sam to release the rope.

The short distance back to the riverbank was ponderous against the current and the wind but eventually, with the aid of a few on the bank pulling on the rope thrown to them, they edged alongside. The onlookers craned their necks for a view of the body and, almost as one, recoiled as it came into view. John was well known to the folk of the city and no doubt the sight of his body in the wooden boat shocked them as it did Bolam. Whispers ran through the gathering.

Grabbing the helpful hand of a bystander, Bolam stepped onto the bank and immediately slipped, his feet gliding on the mud churned up by the crowd. His helper hung on and held fast as Bolam, now on his knees, mud smeared up his legs, used his other hand to grasp a tree root and haul himself ashore. The crowd cleared, almost intuitively. No need for the policeman to order calm or to ask for room.

A stillness, unlike anything Bolam had experienced before, settled across the riverbank as willing hands helped to steady the boat and carefully raise John Mitchell's body off the water and gently onto a tarpaulin laid out on the bank. Bolam bent over the body and carefully moved the arms to its side, straightened its legs and stared hard at the grim face below him.

"What happened to you, John?" he whispered as he gathered John Mitchell's treasured coat around him and gently fastened the buttons, bottom to top, stopping only at the last where one had been lost.

After issuing instructions to the constable and willing helpers, Bolam stepped back to allow the body to be wrapped and transported to the mortuary. He sighed deeply as he watched the men at work. This was not something he was looking forward to. Over the years he'd dealt with all manner of gruesome cases, seen sights that would turn most stomachs, but had always stuck to his task. This was different though, the memory of John and his newborn made it so. Someone needed to answer for this and Bolam grimly swore to himself to make it his mission. Another lad without a father, especially such a proud and loving one, grieved him.

First though, he knew he had another awful job to do and he did not relish it. John Mitchell's house was only half a mile down the riverbank and his wife deserved to be given the news of her husband's death properly.

****

"Come in and sit down, Bolam." Chief Superintendent Charlton's gravelly voice beckoned. Bolam entered the office, the smell of leather and pipe tobacco was hanging in the air. "Terrible business. I'm sorry it was you who had to tell his widow."

Bolam grimaced, remembering the look of horror on the face of Mrs Mitchell when she opened the door to him. Just the mere presence of a policeman at her door spelled trouble and her husband wasn't the sort to be on the wrong side of the law. She clearly knew something serious had happened. Later, after he had left her to grieve, alone with her new-born son, he knew he would never forget that look. It wasn't just horror that looked back at him, it was an inner anguish that confronted him. This, he thought, must have been the look on his mother's face at the pithead on that fateful day.

"I've just had the report from the doctor. Mitchell's death was no accident, he was stabbed." Bolam straightened in his seat. "The doctor found a single stab wound in his lower back, severing the spinal cord. He would have lost control of his legs instantly."

"Was that the only wound?" Bolam questioned.

"The doctor could find nothing else. It looks as if drowning was the cause of death. His lungs were full of water." The superintendent sighed, struck a match and held it over his pipe, drawing deeply. "The report suggests he was tipped into the river after being stabbed. There's mud jammed into his finger nails and one nail is torn, as if he was grasping at the bank."

Bolam looked down at his knees, the mud from that morning's slip was still caked on his trousers. He could see how a paralysed man would have no chance of getting out of the river without help. "Why? What's the motive? John Mitchell was on his way home from work. He didn't even own a watch let alone jewellery. His wife said he never took money to work, so it can't be a robbery."

"If it was a robbery, the robber took everything. There was nothing at all to be found in his clothes. Your guess as to the motive is as good as mine. I've sent out two constables to ask around the pubs tonight, to see if anyone saw or heard anything. I'd like you to lead on this, Frank." Bolam stood tall. The superintendent rarely used his first name. "I've told them to report to you in the morning with what they find."

\*\*\*\*

Two miles away, the collector closed the cupboard door, and smiled to himself.

# August, 1914, Durham, England

The front page of *The Times* on 5 August left no doubt in the mind of the reader.

## Britain at War

Efforts to gain reassurances from the German Government that the neutrality of Belgium would be respected had failed and the night before, at eleven o'clock, the Government of King George V declared war.

Bolam stared down at the newspaper on his desk. He wasn't surprised. The threat of war had been in the air for some time. The sabres had been rattling across Europe and talk of war had been on everyone's lips as the tension mounted. At lunchtime he had heard the singing of 'Rule Britannia' as he walked past the Shakespeare Tavern on Elvert Street. There seemed to be a swell of national pride right through the town.

There was no pride in Bolam's heart though. War or not, he was caught up in his own conflict, fighting a hidden enemy, one he had been hunting for nearly a full year. Except he had no leads. Days and weeks and months had passed without much progress at all. All enquiries came to dead ends. No one had seen John Mitchell after he'd left the cathedral and there was nothing, not even a footprint, to be found on the riverbank. Bolam's frustration grew until another turn of events gave him a sniff of a trail.

A second body had been found in nearby Sacriston a month into the new year, almost exactly six weeks after Bolam had hauled John Mitchell out of the River Wear. James Bell did not return from his morning post round and two days later his body was found by a local farmer's dog in a ditch next to his farm. He'd been stabbed in the lower spine and his throat had been cut. His coat still had his watch and chain fastened to it, he still wore the ring his parents had given him for a twenty-first birthday present and in his pocket were two pennies and a sixpence.

Bolam knew it was the same killer. He sensed it almost immediately. He'd heard other policemen talking about hunches, how their instincts could speak to them about which direction to follow. Now he knew, really knew, what they meant. However, no matter what his instinct told him, the trail was cold almost as quickly as he found it. No clues. Not one.

Since then, two more murders had followed. All within five miles of the city centre, all with the same back injury, all with no clues Bolam could use to find the identity of the killer or their motive. Bolam's frustration was almost at boiling point.

Bolam turned the pages. Over the last year the newspapers had gradually caught on to the possible connections between the four murders. The police had released little, but there was still gossip and by the time the fourth victim had been buried, alarming headlines in all of the local papers, and some national ones, shouted out at their readers that a killer was on the loose in the north east and that no one was safe. More than that, the police were being harassed. What were they doing? Accusations of laziness, incompetence and even a murderer within the ranks were laid out in black and white. Bolam felt the gaze of the public eye burning him as well as the swell of exasperation at the dead ends he continually hit. However, one day, one event, changed all of that.

Now there was only one newspaper story. Pictures of crowds outside Buckingham Palace cheering the king and queen as they waved from the balcony flooded the broadsheet. On the next page there was a report that a German butcher's shop in nearby Crook had been vandalised. Pictures of soldiers returning to barracks, their faces grinning at him from the paper. One soldier, clearly an officer, stood proudly by his horse, a gleaming sword hanging from his belt. The caption read, 'Cavalry keen to catch the Hun'. It was clear that soldiers, trained for war, were now looking forward to doing their job and the days of routine; the marching, the rifle cleaning, the boot and button polishing and the monotony of life in camp would be over.

"Button polishing," Bolam said out loud. The sergeant at the front desk turned his head and looked at him. "Sorry," Bolam said, "just thinking out loud." He picked up the paper and swiftly left the room, taking the stairs to the first floor.

The file room was a tiny, dusty, uncarpeted space filled with three oak filing cabinets. Little swirls of long desiccated particles shimmered in the plumes of light from the single window. Bolam fished into the top drawer of the first cabinet and flicked through the files before lifting one out. He flicked again and found another file before moving to another drawer. Minutes later he left the room with four files.

Back at his desk Bolam opened each file in turn and removed the sheets he wanted. He had collected together the reports for the examination of each of the four murder victims. The documents detailed the doctor's finding in each case and also the other aspects of the examination of the body and clothing. Bolam drew his fountain pen and notepaper from a desk drawer and began to make notes. He was looking for only one thing and began with John Mitchell's file. John Mitchell's coat had had one button missing. Bolam knew this as he had seen it himself, but at the time it meant nothing. Buttons fall off coats all the time.

Moving on, James Bell had been wearing his double-breasted post office issue coat. There was no mention of buttons in the report. Bolam frowned. This wasn't helpful. He had a theory but needed the same luck he'd had in Sunderland to make it work for him.

The third victim, a maid from the County Hotel, had been found in Maiden Castle Woods. The report listed her clothing, all intact except for, according to the examining doctor, a decorative button from her hat seemed to have been ripped off in the attack. It hadn't been found at the scene. Bolam could feel a tinge of excitement growing, but he suppressed it. He needed more than this.

The final report revealed more. The body of a soldier found tucked into bushes at the end of the viaduct near the city's railway station had been wearing the insignia of the local regiment, the Durham Light Infantry. It was noted that his left breast pocket had been ripped off. Bolam knew this meant a brass button was missing as he was very familiar with the uniform, regularly spotting soldiers proudly wearing it in the city.

Three buttons missing from three murder victims: could this be a clue or just coincidence? He knew what the superintendent would say. He needed more, he needed to know what happened to James Bell's coat. He'd not done the leg work and only had reports from officers to go by. Tomorrow he'd take a trip to Sacriston.

\*\*\*\*

Bolam lived alone. At the age of thirty-four he'd only had one romantic relationship but that had come to nothing. Life in the police force, especially for a young detective wanting to make his mark and working long hours, was anti-social. After a year of erratic courtship, he found the love of his life was now someone else's flame and the fire burned both ways. Not a man to get angry or take revenge, Bolam merely walked away and made his job his mistress.

Wednesdays were always quiet but as Bolam arrived at his small house on Church Street, things were different. This was not any ordinary day. Almost everyone was in the street, neighbours gossiping and speculating about the news. Trying to avoid being drawn in, Bolam avoided their eyes, especially his immediate neighbour, Bessie Robinson. If sent to fight the Germans, he imagined she would talk them to death. He chuckled inwardly as he pictured her on a horse with a loudhailer, delivering a dose of the news to the unsuspecting Hun who were in the process of fleeing from her monotonous voice.

"Good evening, Detective." Thankfully, the voice was not the harsh rasp that typically flew from Bessie's mouth.

Reverend Thompstone leaned in to Bolam and whispered. "You thought it was Bessie, didn't you? I saw you cringe." He was right. Bolam had twitched at the first word, expecting the worst. Bolam smiled now.

Since moving to Durham he had struck up a rapport with the clergyman. He'd shared more than a few whiskies with the man and chewed the fat over politics, religion and the good and bad of the British Empire. Despite his obvious religious role, Reverend Thompstone had strong views on all sorts of aspects of life, including the role of women in society, who, according to him, would lead our nation someday. Bolam wasn't so sure, though he knew that women could be as mentally strong as any man. After all his mother had been through, she proudly brought up her family and worked to earn a wage. He had never heard her complain, bemoan her bad luck or take anyone's name in vain. Women like her could lead this country. He was sure of that. But would they ever be given the chance?

"Come in, Edward," Bolam laughed. "I've got a good bottle open." The pair slipped inside, avoiding the gaze of Bessie who was doing her best to catch either's eye.

"That was a close call," the clergyman sighed as the door closed behind them. "You wouldn't believe what I have to listen to after communion every Sunday!"

"Actually, I'd believe anything. I have no idea how her husband sleeps. I can sometimes hear her nagging him through the wall. Goodness knows what she's going to be like now we're at war. There'll be no stopping her. Look, come in, there's something I want to ask you."

\*\*\*\*

23

Bolam woke on the sofa with a thick head. An empty bottle of scotch lay on the floor. The glass beside it glimmered in the sun streaming through the window and he sighed. Between the pair of them, they'd polished off three quarters of a bottle before Edward staggered home to the vicarage. The conversation had twisted and turned through European politics, and the causes of the war, to women's rights and the changing fortunes of the Russian royal family. Thompstone was well read and had contacts in high places, having enjoyed a public school background. He always had a view about whatever was happening in the world.

Bolam had dropped in his question just as the whisky was oiling his friend's tongue. "In your role, you must come across some strange people. Have you ever met anyone with a passion for something, so strong, it consumes them?"

Even with his hangover, Bolam remembered the change in Thompstone. It was as if he'd stuck a pin right into a nerve. He stopped talking and for what seemed like an eternity glared furiously at the flames leaping in the fire grate. Without warning, or even mention of the question, the reverend reverted directly back to the previous topic they'd discussed. At the time, Bolam chose not to push the issue, thinking the spirit had gone to his friend's head, but now, in the morning light, he wondered. What demon had he conjured up inside the vicar's head, what was it that, within an instant, made his blood boil?

As far as Bolam was concerned, he considered Edward a close friend but in reality he really only knew him superficially. A few snippets here and there of his upbringing and family life, but very little depth. They actually were like chalk and cheese. Bolam dragged up and away from a coal face, his friend transported to the north. But from what? Had he fled? Left something behind maybe? Bolam knew sometimes a theological calling was more than a vocation and that people had found solace and a safe haven in the ministry. Was this true for his friend?

His thoughts were shattered by his neighbour. Poor Charlie, he thought to himself. Bessie was clearly giving her husband a good dressing down about something and her ranting voice rasped through the wall like a mechanical drill. Bolam moved to his kitchen and turned on a tap. He needed a cup of tea and a clear head before he could get on with his day. Whatever poor old Charlie had done, he really wasn't bothered. He had other plans.

\*\*\*\*

The road to Sacriston was not an easy ride and Bolam's five year old Raleigh bicycle did not have the gears to deal with the hills of County Durham. The climb out of the city took him a good hour and then the going was relatively flat on Lanchester Road. Cycling past Earl's House, an industrial school; a sort of reform school for boys involved in petty crimes or persistent truancy, Bolam remembered the trip he'd taken with some of the lads on their annual visit to Tynemouth. It was the Reverend Thompstone who'd got him involved. With hindsight Bolam could see that his friend had quickly worked out his passion for helping youngsters, especially those who were thrown a rough deal in life. With some deft manipulation of Bolam's conscience Bolam had become a trustee of the school and occasionally was invited to take part in events, though his work often limited active participation. The Tynemouth trip had opened his eyes even further. Despite their rough backgrounds, he could see the lads were generally good kids.

In fact Bolam had this view of all youngsters and he regularly reminded the local bobbies when they moaned about them, that children were only as good as those who led them, taught them or trained them. These lads were no different to him really. Yes, they'd made some serious mistakes but he felt all of them were redeemable. Since the beginning of time youngsters had challenged the world of adults. Some went too far and broke the law.

On that trip, one lad, a tall muscular twelve-year-old in his final year, with skin hardened from working on the school's farm and hair like the straw he harvested, confided in Bolam that he'd stolen from the local butcher purely to escape his drunkard of a father who beat him and his sister regularly. His sister, older by five years, often tried to protect him but had been married off to a local farmer, so the beatings intensified for the boy. Bolam, taken by the lad's story, thinking he saw something of himself in the boy, went out of his way to help him find a job. The last he'd heard about Arnold Wilson was he was doing well as a labourer with the stonemasons.

The Bell house was right at the edge of the village, just opposite the school. It was a yellow brick ex-miner's cottage set at the end of a terrace. Newly washed clothes hung on the line, billowing in the gentle breeze, and a small boy sat on the wall, kicking the iron-clad heels of boots far too big for him against the brickwork, shooting the odd spark here and there. Bolam dismounted, pushed the bicycle over to the wall and smiled. "Hello, son, is your mam in?"

The boy stopped kicking his feet and slowly looked the policeman up and down. Without saying a word the boy swivelled his backside on the wall, slid down into the yard and ducked under the washing. "Maaa," Bolam heard the boy shout, "there's a polliss oot the front." his broad accent almost singing the message to his mother. This made Bolam chuckle to himself. As a lad he'd have sounded the same, but since his promotion he'd deliberately clipped his accent and use of colloquialisms. It was made clear to him by his superiors that if he was to move into even higher circles he'd need to ensure they could understand him. After all his mother had been through, she proudly brought up her family and worked to earn a wage.

"Mrs Bell?" Bolam asked.

"Aye, and who are you?"

"My name's Bolam, Mrs Bell. Detective Constable Bolam. I've come to ask you about your husband."

"I told the others all I know, there's nowt else to say." Her voice was steely, though he detected a slight wobble. Clearly her husband's death was still very raw.

"I'm now investigating the case, Mrs Bell. I'd just like to ask you something else if I can."

Like the boy had done, his mother scanned Bolam, as if she was the policeman and he a suspect, and then fixed his eyes with hers. There was a force in them. Bolam remembered his mother, remembered her inner steel as he grew up. "Will it help? Will it bring him back? Will it pay the bloody bills? Tell me, Detective, will it bring my man back?" Her voice, even, but crackling with inner fury and grief, threw these words at Bolam and he could tell she was forcing her tears back, too proud to cry. Certainly not in front of him or her son. Only in the darkness.

Only once as a boy did he hear his mother cry. He'd been woken by a storm and in between the howls of the wind and the pattering rain on his bedroom window he'd caught the distinct sound of grief. In the room next to his, he heard his mother trying to stifle her tears and he listened to her helplessly, before drifting back to sleep not knowing what to do. He'd never mentioned it to her or anyone other than the Reverend Thompstone, when, worse for a few glasses of beer, he'd let his guard down and emotions poured out. He hadn't realised how much his father's death had really affected him.

"I want to catch him, Mrs Bell. I can't make things better, but I can catch him, and I need help."

Again she looked at him carefully, scrutinising him as a watchmaker might inspect his creations, and after what seemed like minutes, turned away from him, back between the washing. "You'd better come in then," she said. Bolam needed no more prompting and followed.

The inside of the house was warm and smelled of coal smoke. They'd entered into the kitchen and a fire glowed brightly in a cast iron range. A black steel kettle sat on the hot plate, steam curling from its spout. More washing was drying over a clotheshorse and a fresh batch sat in a poss tub near a stone sink. This was clearly the kitchen of a house-proud woman.

"Sit down." Her tone was clipped but she beckoned to a wooden chair adjacent to the grate. Bolam imagined her husband in the chair after a long cold shift, warming his feet against the grate. Not wishing to offend, he eased himself down and sat. Mrs Bell stood, silently facing him, clearly waiting for him to speak.

"According to the case file," he began, reading the signal, "your husband was wearing his coat when they

28

found him?" Mrs Bell said nothing but nodded slightly giving Bolam leave to carry on. "I wonder if you kept the coat? The report says nothing about it other than what was in the pockets. I think it might be possible it can give me a clue."

Without response Mrs Bell left the room through a door behind the detective, her heels clicking on the stone floor. Bolam heard her climb the stairs and picked up movement in the rooms above, then quick feet on the stairs again before her heels clicked back into the kitchen. She stood in front of Bolam, a navy blue greatcoat held by the shoulders dangled in front of her. "I've not got the heart to throw his clothes out," she whispered, and tears began to roll down her cheeks. "Catch him. Just catch him."

Bolam stared at the coat. The middle button on the left side was missing.

\*\*\*\*

It was Friday before he was able to talk to the boss. He felt he'd hardly slept after returning from Sacriston and the feeling had built as the week went on. The combination of Mrs Bell's grief and the missing button made his brain whirl at night. Such a proud woman, clearly doing her best to bring up a fatherless child. A fatherless child. Another one.

How many fatherless children might there be in a year's time Bolam wondered? People were full of optimism and talking of a victory by Christmas, but talk and smiles didn't win wars, men did. Living men, wounded men and dead men. There would be a price to pay.

James Bell had already paid his dues and Bolam had made his promise to his widow, as if he needed a further reason to catch this killer. Through her tears she saw his sincerity and through her sobs she heard his resolve. He would do everything to bring her husband's killer to justice. But her gaunt face still haunted him through the night. Her face, the button, the missing button, the missing buttons, her face, John Mitchell...

A kaleidoscope of thoughts and images he could not stem or make sense of. They swept in and out, mixed with images of war. Men on horses, glistening in polished steel and gilt, rode into Durham led by Mrs Bell cradling John Mitchell's baby on her knee. Crowds of children dressed in black stood solemnly while they passed and hooves clattered over the cobbled streets as the column progressed up Saddler Street towards the cathedral. The masons were waiting for them, massed in ranks, standing in rows, like soldiers against the north wall, chisels and mallets in their hands. The children had somehow beaten the riders to the top of the hill and stood adjacent to the masons, still silent, still solemn.

The mounted horses, now led by Bolam himself, trotted directly towards them and at Bolam's command halted in perfect unison. At that moment the buttons from the tunics of all mounted men shot from their stitching and flew upwards creating a hail of shining metal that chinked and rattled melodically on the paths and gravestones, bouncing off the heads and chests of the masons and children. The earth surrounding the great building began to shake. Cracks appeared in the north wall and masonry started to crumble and fall.

Bolam sat up in bed, wet with sweat. It was early on Thursday morning and he still had a day to wait. If he had slept, he could not remember doing so and it seemed any rest that had come his way was abruptly interrupted by the same demons that had tortured him throughout the week. Even so, it wasn't a tired man that went to work that morning and he spent the early hours with purpose, preparing his thoughts to present to Charlton.

Having put his thoughts onto paper Bolam dozed off quickly that night, seemingly having cleared his mind, and woke on Friday to a bright warm day. The Durham streets were still full of the national pride and optimism that started earlier in the week. Field Marshall Lord Kitchener's face seemed to be everywhere. His huge claw-like moustache seemed to grab at Bolam as he walked by, while his eyes and pointing finger followed him into the distance. The newly appointed Secretary of State for War left you with no uncertainty. The posters clung to billboards, windows and walls throughout the town. It was almost a relay of messages from one street corner to another.

'Your Country Needs You'

Not today, thought Bolam, the people of County Durham come first. The morning's paper talked of nothing but war. Bolam's eyes however, saw none of this. The meeting with his superior was the only thing on his mind.

****

The time ticked on slowly until half past ten. He couldn't get Mrs Bell's face from his mind and twisted visions from his dreams began to return. The case was

31

nibbling at him constantly, always there, always prodding his mind. He knew he was becoming unhealthily obsessed with it but repeatedly justified his state by reassuring himself that it was his job to be this bothered by crime.

Trying to clear his head, Bolam sat at his desk, repeatedly filling his pen and draining the ink into round pools on his blotting paper. In front of him was his report. His theory. His plan. Bolam watched the clock hands move past every minute until Chief Superintendent Charlton arrived. "Frank. Good morning." The greeting was mixed. Another informal use of his name but this time curbed by a formal greeting, weighted in a manner that instantly told Bolan it was anything but a 'good morning'.

"Morning, sir," Bolam replied. "I think I have got something on our murder cases. Something that links them together." He instantly regretted his words. His enthusiasm had run away with itself. He'd read the signs but not curbed his tongue and inwardly cursed himself.

"I see." His boss's tone hadn't changed. If anything it had hardened. "You'd better come up to my office then."

Bolam followed, cursing himself again. Why had he not just waited? He might have gained promotion because of this man but he also knew his mood defined the weather in the station. His temper was legendary and Bolam had witnessed his boss's thunder, crockery flying and chairs upturned over seemingly trivial matters. He steeled himself for the next exchange.

"Come in, Bolam." There was no invite to sit. Charlton slowly removed his coat and his hat then carefully hung them on the mahogany stand in the corner of the room. He straightened his coat and reached into the pocket, removing a pipe and a packet of Swan Vesta matches. He sat, his desk forming a barrier between the men, and carefully removed a match and flicked it onto the desk. "You don't smoke, Bolam, do you?" It was a rhetorical question, Bolam's boss knew too well his officer didn't have the same affection for tobacco as he did. "Ever tried?"

"Only once, sir. I didn't really take to it." In fact he'd almost been sick. As a youngster his uncle, home from a long shift underground, had stuck a lit cigarette in his mouth and instructed him to breathe in. Despite his uncle's obvious entertainment from his coughing fit and queasiness, he failed to see the joke and the thought of trying it again had never entered his head.

"Strange thing. I see you as a thinker, Bolam, a man who likes to ponder. Nothing better than a pipe to help you do that." As if he needed support, Charlton tapped his pipe in the air, pointing the stem towards Bolam. Not waiting for a reply he retrieved the match and struck it, sweeping it up to his pipe simultaneously reached his mouth. He took three long draws and then dropped the match to the floor, grinding it into the oak floor board with his boot. "So, what have you got to tell me?"

Bolam carefully raised his report and spoke. He explained the events of the previous few days, his scrutiny of the files, his ride to Sacriston, even his sleepless nights, but not his dreams. He did everything in his power to curb his passion for this case before announcing his theory. "Sir," he paused. "Sir, I think this case has a motive. You might think it's a strange one but I cannot find any other reason for the four murders. I can link them in the way the murderer used his knife but I have found something new. In fact they all share one similarity that I believe is the motive." He paused again, breathing deeply. "I think the murderer collects buttons, sir."

Chief Superintendent Charlton removed his pipe from his mouth, eased his chair back from the desk and slowly stood. He turned and looked out of the window at the street below. The silence ached and Bolam, uncertain of his ground decided to keep his mouth shut. After what seemed like several minutes, the tension was broken.

"See that Bolam?" Charlton pointed the pipe at the scene. "The people down there, they're at war. We're at war. I'm at war. You hear that?" His voice was now rising. "I'm being seconded to the army. Leaving tomorrow. Apparently they need a man like me in the DLI and I am, according to the council, more than happy to help." The silence erupted again and Bolam knew that the meeting was over.

Unexpectedly, Charlton stepped smartly around his desk and opened the door. "Thank you, Bolam," he said in a clipped tone. "You'll need to take the lead here. They aren't replacing me. I suggest you concentrate on the little things instead of fanciful theories. The men will need strong leadership while I'm gone. The routines and rotas need to run smoothly. I like a well-oiled machine as you know and in my absence I expect no less from you."

"Sir," Bolam began but his words were harshly chopped short.

"I've left a list of instructions downstairs in the office for you." The tone was now mechanical. The stress behind Charlton's words was almost physical. "Goodbye, Bolam." Charlton quivered the door a little and stepped forward slightly, indicating very clearly the expectation that it was time for his officer to leave the room without any further discourse.

Bolam, lost for words and clearly commanded to be silent, smiled benignly and left the room. The door closed swiftly behind him and he paused on the landing to draw breath. Behind the door he heard a loud sigh followed by an exclamation, "Bastards!" Then silence. Bolam shrugged and headed downstairs.

****

The rest of the day went as slowly as it had started. Bolam struggled to motivate himself before plodding home through the wind that had whipped up. He'd read Charlton's list. It was six pages of instructions that simply placed Bolam as caretaker. Nothing was to be changed, nothing new and certainly nothing in the way of generating any additional work. Each paragraph detailed in minute detail how Charlton wanted things done. Bolam knew his boss was a perfectionist and had thought that he was trusted by him, but this document made it clear to Bolam that he wasn't and that no one else was either. Even the procedures and routines Bolam knew inside out were listed and broken down into basics. By the end of the last page, Bolam felt not only disheartened but deeply disturbed.

The wind stung his face and blew leaves in small eddies that danced annoyingly in front of him as he slowly climbed the street to his small home. The gloomy evening followed him into the house. Instead of the fire he'd felt in his belly over the past few days, he sat alone in the dark, deep in a whirl of thoughts conspiring against him. His boss had nailed the coffin firmly shut on the deaths of four locals and was shipping out to France. All very well for him, leaving Bolam to hold the fort and to keep the place ticking over. He might be gone for months, maybe longer.

All very well for him, away at the war, while people still lived and died back home. How could he expect Bolam just to be a watchman for the place with no remit to solve these awful crimes? It wasn't like the locals and newspapers had been quiet about the lack of police progress. He couldn't imagine that a war in Europe was going to stop that. And worse, by the time Charlton returned, if he survived, it could be too late. And goodness knows if more people would suffer the same fate. Bolam stared through the grey at the empty fire hearth.

"If he survives," he whispered. "When he returns."

Bolam moved from his chair to the hearth, kneeling in front of the fire grate. He plucked the poker from its holder, a brass tube with a rough owl shaped motif on it, and set about raking the ash in the grate. After he was satisfied, he removed the cover below the grate and withdrew the dustpan from the opening, careful not to disturb the heap of ash he'd created. Concentrating on keeping it level, he stood up, clutching the dustpan, and slowly walked through the room into the back kitchen and then out though the door into the yard. Moments later he returned to the hearth with an empty dustpan having emptied the contents in the bin in the yard. Later in the week, they'd be collected and used in communal ash toilets, or 'netties' as the locals called them, like the ones next to his mother's street. Bolam felt lucky he had a water closet in an outhouse set in his yard.

At the hearth he leaned to his right and opened a wooden box set to one side of the fireplace and took out several sheets of newspaper and half a dozen sticks. He quickly laid these into the fire grate and balanced some thicker sticks on top before taking a small shovelful of coal from the box and wrapping it in newspaper to form a parcel. This he gently placed on top of the sticks. His well-rehearsed routine was the system he'd learned from his mother and it never failed. He struck a match and lit the newspaper. The flames licked at the sticks and the room filled with flashes of yellow light, slowly building warmth as the flames grew.

"If he returns." Bolam sat back, stared at the flames and smiled. "He'll never know."

\*\*\*\*

Saturday arrived and brought rain. Bolam found sleep difficult to come by, and again, once asleep took haunted by images of his case with him, unable to switch his mind off even in slumber. He'd woken at around midnight, disturbed by a pair of cats disputing territory in the street. Again his thoughts spiralled but this time he began to let his mind run freely, not trying to suppress them. It was a simple decision not to fight the inevitable and at the same time he began hoping for an opening. Eventually he dozed off and slept deeply.

He rose at nine, which for him was unusual, even on a day off. His internal clock usually woke him at six, but not today. He breakfasted on kippers and buttered toast, a treat he kept for his one day a week off. The fishmonger in the town had a reliable supply of freshly smoked fish from Craster, locally thought to be the best in Britain. Bolam was just finishing his last mouthful when a knock on the door broke the silence. He quickly swallowed and made his way from the small kitchen along a short passageway to welcome his visitor.

"My Lord, it stinks in here, Frank. We're supposed to be catching fish today not making fertiliser with them!"

The Reverend Edward Thompstone beamed as he stepped in. "Come on my boy, let's get going. I hear there's a possibility of a run on today."

Twenty minutes later the two friends were on a mission. Salmon. To Bolam, the king of fish. As a boy he'd watched them leap improbable heights over rocks, weirs and other barriers on their quest to swim upstream to reproduce. He was enchanted by their perseverance, their effort and determination to succeed. They'd swum hundreds of miles of open ocean before entering the river and never ever gave up in their singular mission. He'd sworn to himself that one day he'd catch one. Until he'd met Thompstone he'd never tried, but the reverend introduced him to the art of fly-fishing and now every August Bolam looked forward to the arrival of his quarry in the Wear. Today, Bolam sensed, was going to be a good day.

Four hours of whipping a fly rod had Bolam's right bicep burning. It didn't wipe the smile off his face though. Two glistening seven-pound salmon lay in the bottom of the rowing boat, one each. There might have been even more of a catch but Bolam had lost what he thought was going to be a monster. "Probably a minnow." Thompstone laughed when it slipped Bolam's hook. The day had indeed been good and Bolam felt he'd relaxed for the first time in weeks. Even the constant rain hadn't dampened his spirits, although his friend's parting words hit him hard.

"See you in church tomorrow, Frank. It'll be my last service for a while." Bolam looked at his friend, puzzled. "I've joined up. Kitchener's been pointing at me right out of those posters and I realised I had to go. Men in war need a sympathetic ear, maybe even God."

There was a long silence as Bolam's heart sank. "When do you leave?" he asked.

"Tomorrow night, right after the service. No rest for the wicked, eh?"

The joke went unanswered. Bolam managed a few short parting words and they went their separate ways. The climb back up the street to his house seemed mountainous to Bolam, but on reaching the summit, his mind was made up. The salmon had not only taken his fly but they'd inspired him. He wasn't about to give up either. He might be losing his only real friend in the town, but he would make it his mission to catch the murderer that plagued his mind and had caused so much grief. Outside his front door he felt his passion return. No matter how many barriers he had to cross, no matter where he had to go or what got in his way he would catch this killer.

# January, 1915, Durham, England

The war had not ended at Christmas as the newspapers predicted, despite the reports of an unofficial truce in no man's land on Christmas Day. Early optimism had turned to a hardened sense that this was going to be a long attritional campaign. On the home front people were scared, not just due to stories of the horrors of the new mechanised and chemical warfare being played out in France and Belgium, but because they realised they were vulnerable too. German battleships had bombed ports in the north of England, killing over a hundred people. Slightly further south, Zeppelin bombing had killed again on the East Anglian coast. Men expressed their concern by enlisting in their hundreds, many forming new regiments, nicknamed 'Pals' because so many had signed up together from the same areas.

No one was more concerned than Bolam. His mother, sister and his sister's family lived in Seaham, just sixteen miles from one of the destructive raids. The war was suddenly very real, as the realisation that Germany could reach into England and spread amongst the population. Bolam had visited his family. Returning to his roots brought back vivid memories of his childhood. Little had changed. The rows of terraced cottages running parallel with the road to the mine, the slag heaps graphically illustrating the toil of those underground, the blackened faces of the men returning home. In her front room, his mother, in her sixties now, did her best to hide her fear.

Women in mining communities were good at hiding such emotions, never knowing whether their husbands and sons would return from the depths. But he could see through it. His sister, now living only two doors away with a young family and a miner for a husband, unusually, hid nothing. Bolam wondered if the combination of the coal face and the Western Front had gotten to her. The fear in her eyes was plainly evident. "I worry about him every day. I didn't expect to have the same worries about sending the kids to school."

The second thing playing on Bolam's mind was the murder case. In the six months since Charlton had left him in charge, he'd made no progress on the case. Every avenue he went down was yet another dead end and the case still plagued him. He still allowed the details to flow at night and, while he slept better, it was punctuated with periods of wakefulness, when snippets of everything he'd discovered were juggled and rearranged in his mind.

Another thing that puzzled him was the timeframe. The four murders had all happened within a matter of months, yet seven months later, not a single report of anything similar. He'd contacted neighbouring police forces, and after speculating that local industry might be a link, his enquiries ventured as far afield as Nottinghamshire and Leicestershire, other coal mining areas. The more he pondered, the more frustrated he became. Surely there was something he was missing and he could not get this nagging thought out of his mind.

The morning's newspaper headlines reported news of a battle in the North Sea near Dogger Bank where the

Navy had sunk a German battleship. The station was alive with optimism when Bolam arrived. After the horror expressed about recent casualties down the coast, the mood had turned with this news and the constable on duty at the front desk was singing as Bolam arrived.

"Rule Britannia. Britannia rules the waves. Britons never, never, never, will be slaves."

"Something cheered you up, George?" Bolam tapped the constable on the shoulder as he passed by.

"Have you not seen the headlines, Detective? We've given the Hun what for in the North Sea. That'll teach them to come over here with their big guns." The constable swiped a punch towards an invisible foe as he spoke.

"You know what they say, George, one battle doesn't win a war. So much for the papers saying it would be over soon. I can't see anything stopping it." Bolam sat down at a desk behind the constable and began pouring himself a cup of tea from the pot on the nearby stove. "This war is just starting, and not just in France and Belgium, I hear there are conflicts growing all over Europe and what's more I read there are even soldiers from India involved now."

"You're probably right, sir. I bumped into Harry Pattison the other day. He'd been shot through the arm in France and sent home. He showed me a curved dagger he'd been given by an Indian sergeant he'd met out there. Beautiful piece of work. It was about ten inches long and the hilt was carved and polished. There were elephants, tigers and all manner of animals on it. Goodness knows how long it took to make. I expect there are all sorts of odd things out there you can pick up."

Bolam nearly choked on his first slurp of tea.

"You all right, Detective?"

Bolam's eyes were streaming and he was struggling to put his drink down on the desk without spilling it. "I'm fine, George," spluttered Bolam, wiping a stream of hot liquid from his chin. "I just coughed as I was drinking."

Bolam stood up and paced to the end of the room and back to the front window, dabbing at his face with his sleeve. George watched, as his boss tapped out a rhythm on the window frame. In the street, people milled about their business, heading for work, some already at work, others going about daily chores. He could see one of his men arriving for his shift and watched as he was stopped in his tracks by a soldier that had just rounded the corner into the street. The pair shook hands. Clearly they knew each other and talked for a while before parting. Probably another man on leave from the front.

"A dagger you say, George?" Bolam turned to face the constable.

"Yes sir. It looked grand. Real shiny with a lion's head on the scabbard. I wouldn't mind one myself. Apparently he had an Indian coin as well. A rupee I think he called it. He said his younger brother collects coins and this would be a real present for him. Something a bit different. He even said there are Chinese folk out there so he's planning on getting him one of their coins if he can." George smiled at his boss. "Are you sure you are all right, sir? You look a bit pale if you don't mind me saying so."

"No, I'm fine, George. I nearly choked on my tea there though. Completely went down the wrong way."

Choking however, was not the thing on Bolam's mind. An idea had just formed in his head and he needed to test it out.

****

The Headquarters of the Durham Light Infantry was an unimposing building but on entering through the oak door into a wood panelled foyer, Bolam was instantly aware of the sense of history in this place. He'd taken nearly an hour and a half cycling across country to the place and was slightly out of breath and the awe he experienced on entry didn't help his condition. The plaques adorning the walls commemorated the various conflicts and countries the regiment had served in, including a very fine trophy celebrating the DLI's successes on the polo field in India. Bolam drew a deep breath and walked over to the desk in the corner of the foyer. Showing his identification to a man in uniform sporting a bushy moustache, he made his request.

Clearly the man was one of few words. "Sit over there." He said pointing to a row of chairs against the opposite wall. "Someone will help you."

Bolam thanked the man and did as instructed, and once sat down, noticed that the man had left his station. Opposite him was a huge oil painting of a group of red-coated soldiers athletically charging with fixed bayonets. The picture astonished Bolam. Given the number of khaki uniforms he'd seen recently, he wondered why bright red had been ever worn. Surely a man wearing red would stand out against most backgrounds, as opposed to one in a drab brown or green who would have more chance of going unnoticed.

Bolam's thoughts were interrupted by a second uniformed man, this time much taller and clean shaven. His left sleeve was pinned back at the elbow, suggesting an amputation. "If you'll step this way, Detective, I'll see if I can help you."

The soldier led Bolam into an adjacent office and introduced himself as Captain James. "Now what can I do for you, Detective?" he asked.

Bolam explained the reasoning behind his visit and made his request. "I wonder if I can see a list of all of the recruits into the DLI since August?"

Captain James raised his eyebrows. "All of the recruits you say? Do you have any idea how many that might be?" It was clear from Bolam's face he didn't. "There are hundreds. Are you sure?"

Bolam sat up straight. "This is my only way forward, Captain, I have no choice. I would be grateful for your help."

Twenty minutes later Bolam was opening the third of five large leather bound books. Each contained the actual recruitment documents for every man who had signed up to fight. He'd already found Chief Superintendent Charlton's papers and was amused to learn that his middle name was Mary. Clearly a family name, but nevertheless a name that was not the most appropriate for his boss. Bolam imagined what fun the constables would have with it if they found out and struggled to force a smirk off his face. Two sheets later he came across Edward's paperwork.

Captain James was right. There were indeed hundreds. Bolam had originally planned to write every name down and then study them back at the police station, but he realised now that because of the sheer numbers he was wasting his time. He recognised a few names, mostly locals he knew and one or two petty criminals he'd arrested. One name did stand out though, and his heart sank. Arnold Wilson. Judging by the paperwork, if it was indeed the lad he'd rescued from Earl's House, he'd lied about his age. Arnold would only be around sixteen and yet he'd signed up as a nineteen-year-old to join a man's war. Such was the pressure on men to do the right thing. "My God, I hope he survives," Bolam murmured.

Placing the last volume on top of the other four, Bolam sat back and stared at the pile. He'd stopped counting after he had reached two hundred. Nothing. "Another bloody dead end," he whispered to himself. He was no further forward. It was like looking for a needle in a haystack. His theory had been blocked. If, as he had thought, the murderer had taken the King's shilling, then surely something would have stood out. He wasn't exactly sure what he was expecting to see but he knew his idea had mileage.

Bolam thanked the Captain and left his office, back into the foyer. The desk was empty and each step Bolam took echoed. Pausing before he pushed the door to exit he turned. The red of the painting hit him. It overpowered the room and seemed to invade his very space. There was no way you could enter this room and not be aware of those gallant charging soldiers. Not like today's uniforms.

"Not like today's uniforms," Bolam almost gasped. "Not like the uniforms of the men who had just signed up. They would all just blend in. Where better than the carnage of war to hide if you are a murderer? Who'd notice you?" He paused, and thought of the conversation with his constable earlier that day. "And who'd notice a killer who collected memorabilia of his conquests in such turmoil?" Bolam paused again, took one last look at the redcoats and left. He might not have found his man from the records but he now knew in his heart he was right, and he also knew exactly what he had to do.

# 24th April, 1915, Ypres, Belgium

Second Lieutenant Bolam sat back against the wooden bench at the rear of the *estaminet*. He'd arrived in Poperinge, an hour ago. His first posting was to take charge of a small platoon of men somewhere south east of Ypres and this was his last chance for any form of rest before his move to the front tomorrow. This was a different world. Men from all over Britain and beyond mixed here despite the fact the town was shelled regularly. The wall his bench lent against had clearly been patched up several times. Yet this was a place where those weary of the war had a short time to enjoy some form of comfort. A beer, some decent food, a bath, a woman maybe. He could see evidence of the latter playing out in front of him as a Tommy disappeared up the wooden stairs to the first floor with a pretty girl. It was just over two months since he volunteered and left Durham behind. It seemed a long time ago.

Bolam's cycle ride back to the police station from the DLI headquarters had given him thinking time. The plan he'd formed would have been unthinkable only a few months ago. It was extreme, but he knew something extraordinary would have to be done to catch his killer. He needed to stop the dreams and above all he needed to do it for the kids left without fathers.

He could not imagine his old boss agreeing to it. In fact, he could understand why. After all, he had no actual evidence that his quarry was in the Ypres area, just an idea based on several pieces of flimsy evidence. The length of time without a murder suggested some form of disappearance, the number of northern regiments in Belgium and the potential for someone to get their hands on all sorts of interesting shiny and interesting artefacts. There'd be buttons and medals galore out there!

In Bolam's mind this was enough. He wasn't prepared to sit and wait any longer. Even so, he'd nearly backed out several times before signing on the line at the recruiting office. Yet two days later when he sat the next most senior police officer at the station down and told him that from tomorrow he'd be in charge, it seemed the perfectly natural thing to do. In fact he was quite surprised how easily he lied to the man, telling him he'd been specifically requested to join Charlton 'out there'. He was equally surprised he didn't have to field any questions. Clearly the notion of men going to war was such a day-to-day occurrence that not one person questioned his motive. Putting his name to paper was where the idea became reality and he knew he needed to ensure he remained focused and resolute.

He'd slept well that night. His rest at night had been so disturbed and erratic since the beginning of this case. Every time he thought he'd got some way to gaining control over his thoughts, another twist seemed to derail his ability to switch off. This time however, he felt different. Gone were the demons that kept returning to wake him, haunting his thoughts in the dead of the night. He awoke with a spring in his step and after a swift breakfast remembered the morning before.

He had ridden directly to the local recruitment office. After queuing for twenty minutes or so behind a group of grinning friends signing up together, it was a swift procedure. The recruiting sergeant looked him up and down then without a word passed him to another soldier sitting at a desk. The soldier, like the sergeant, also sized Bolam up and clearly recognised him, though nothing was said at that point. After taking down Bolam's details, he was sent along a corridor to a small room, asked to strip, and was examined by a medical officer. After being weighed and measured, he was told he could put his clothes back on. "I wish they were all like you," the doctor had said. "It would make my life a bit easier." Bolam had been pleased with this. He'd always been fit and cycling regularly meant that his legs were always strong.

As he was sitting tying his bootlaces, the soldier from the desk entered the room, clearly with something to say. Bolam looked up. "I thought it was you, Mr Bolam," he'd said. "You'll not remember me though, I was only a bairn when you used to come to Earl's House. The name's Billy." The young soldier seemed almost embarrassed, "Billy Johnson."

To Bolam, he still looked a bairn! The young face looked familiar, but the name didn't ring a bell. Nevertheless Bolam had made small talk. The lad, it seemed, due to just surviving pneumonia as a child, was deemed unfit for front line duties and was doing his bit from behind a desk. Clearly Bolam had made an impact on him as it appeared the sergeant wanted a word with him.

"Billy tells me you're a policeman, Mr Bolam." Bolam nodded, wondering where the conversation would lead. "He says you're a detective, and a good bloke. Say's you've helped a lot of kids like him."

"That's nice of the lad. I like to think I do my best for people" Bolam had replied modestly.

It appeared the sergeant had plans for Bolam. Officer training. "The lads at the front need leaders, Mr Bolam. Not your toffee nosed stuck up wealthy folks who get to be officers because of the school they went to. Real men. Men who know how to deal with men and how to get the best out of them. I've been out there and I know the lads need proper leadership. Not people who sneer at them because they've had their hands roughened from work on farms or in quarries or down mines."

Bolam was sent home with his papers. He would attend officer training in Cambridge and would leave by train in three days. There was no discussion. The sergeant had made it clear to Bolam that this was his duty and he would see to it that there would be no dilly-dallying about getting him out to the front line. "These local lads need you, Mr Bolam," he'd said before Bolam could clamber back onto his bicycle.

Training was intense and despite the fact Bolam didn't fit in socially, he made an impact with those in charge for his fitness and clear thinking under pressure. His mother had warned him to be wary of other trainee officers when he visited her and his sister the day before his departure. "Don't think you'll get respect, son," she said. "It's them and us and always will be." She was right so far and his peers, while reasonably polite, did little to make him feel welcome.

However, Bolam was already a man above his station, a constable promoted to detective and now an officer in the Durham Light Infantry. He'd taken the jibes from his friends and the cold shoulders from the educated elite and the higher-ranking police officers he encountered. Bolam knew his strengths and he made it his business to be the best he could be. With his thirst for knowledge, he rapidly honed his map reading skills, learned the new tactics of machine gun deployment and trench warfare.

Above all, he learned how out of touch much of the training was, as the older officers in charge far too often harked back to bygone battles in Africa or India where cavalry charges were used to great effect. Bolam knew the mechanisation of warfare spelled the future. He was soon to find out just how much of an impact these new technologies could have.

Towards the end of his training he was taken to one side by a battle hardened sergeant major who had been training the future officers in the delicate art of trench building. A veteran of campaigns in Africa and the first days of the British Expeditionary Force in France in 1914, he'd been shot through the left hip and now walked with a marked limp.

"Mr Bolam, d'y' mind if I give y' some advice before y' leave us, sir?" Bolam almost didn't realise he was being spoken to. Here was a man from the same part of the world as himself, a man who'd grown up in similar working class conditions and had seen much more of life than he had, and he was asking permission to speak. It seemed wrong, but Bolam knew he was now a member of a different part of the team, although a slightly unwelcome one. If there hadn't been a war on, there would never be a chance that men like himself could become officers. He was under no illusion, his commission was only a temporary affair. At the end of the war, he would have no future in the army, even if he wanted it. He moved closer to the older man.

"All this they're teaching y' here, Mr Bolam, all this new knowledge they're giving y', none of it will matter out there unless y' have the men on y' side. That's something they cannet teach y'. The' think they can, but I've seen officers from here lose the men. And in battle, y' don't want that, y' need them by your side, following y'."

The sergeant major looked around, checking no one else was listening. There was no doubt that this was a speech aimed only at Bolam. "And I'll tell y' this. I've known officers who were a danger to their own men and deserved to be killed, and some were, if you get my drift." His grey eyes peered into Bolam's. "Above anything, Mr Bolam, y' will have a matter of days to get to know y' men, find out something about every one of them, what makes them tick. Learn how to make them laugh and show them the skills y' have. And remember, y' are not one of them, no matter where y' come from and where y' grew up. Y're an officer, a gentleman now, sir. Get this right and y' men will follow y' into Hell itself."

Bolam was about to reply but before he could, the sergeant major brought himself to attention and saluted him. "Good luck, sir," he breathed, then turned and marched away.

"Thank you," Bolam whispered. He looked up at the sky. A flock of starlings were swirling in bewildering formations in the early evening light. They danced and darted like swirling torrents, narrowly missing each other but in perfect harmony. Bolam thought, if only humans could be so carefree, so perfectly balanced, in tune with the world. Would we be in such a predicament? Would he be heading for Belgium? Would he be hunting a killer?

Bolam sipped his beer. It did indeed seem a long time since he left Durham. The train from Cambridge to London, and then to Dover. It had been a rough crossing in the coal barge converted for troop carrying and he'd been sick several times. He wasn't the first to be ill, but once one man started vomiting and the smell of his bile hit the air, sickness moved through the men like the waves they were being tossed around by. Man after man deposited the contents of their stomachs over the side, onto the floor and even onto each other. The sea paid no respect for rank or social class. By the time they'd reached port it seemed like everyone aboard had been retching for the best part of the crossing.

Arriving in Dunkirk he was surprised to find that his next transport was a London bus. It seemed the army was making use of every possible type of vehicle. The bus passed along cobbled streets alongside trucks and bicycles, all overtaking lines of marching troops, horse drawn carriages and carts pulled by oxen. Almost immediately, he was aware of the difference only twenty-two miles of water made between countries. The language, the fields and the buildings were all so unusual to him and the different styles of dress worn by ordinary people stood out as he was driven further into the French countryside and then into Belgium.

Arriving in Poperinge, just to the west of Ypres, Bolam had clambered off the bus and onto the cobbled street. The strong acrid scent of horse manure and engine fumes hit his nose. His vehicle, solely occupied by junior officers like himself, had been at the front of a convoy of four others, all laden with troops and all swarming onto

54

the streets of this small Belgium town. Beyond the smell, the noise assaulted his hearing too. A cacophony of clattering horses' hooves, engines rattling and non-commissioned officers barking orders at the new arrivals seemed to envelop him. Bolam and his fellow officers were met by a young corporal who guided them to a house behind the main street; their sanctuary for the night.

"Are you going to eat at Skindles?" A tall thin officer perched on the edge of the adjacent bed looked up at him while fiddling with his tie. Bolam, completely confused by the question, mumbled a non-committal response. Clearly sensing the confusion the officer carried on, "You know old chap, Skindles, the Officers' Club in Pop. All of the other chaps will be going there."

"I think I'll just have a walk first." Bolam deflected the question. "I'd like to get a feel for the place you know. See the lay of the land." In fact, Bolam had no intention of heading for the Officers' Club, but felt it was better to make an excuse. He was here for more than one purpose and wanted to get a feel for the place. While he could see why he should fraternise with his fellow officers and take what might be the last opportunity to relax for some time, he constantly thought of the killer he sought, his victims and their loved ones. His investigation was beginning again in a foreign land and he felt he should waste no time.

After his companion had left, he stepped out into the night air and after a short walk followed three soldiers into the *estaminet* – a Belgian version of the pubs back home. He'd heard the men talking about them before the boat had left, though any excitement about the promise of beer had been quickly swept away once they'd hit the open sea.

He ordered some food and a dark beer which was sweet and strong, unlike anything Bolam had ever tasted.

In fact, the scene before him was also a revelation to him. A hustle and bustle of soldiers, the odd local and a few women; some serving drinks, others serving the men. Bolam reminded himself of why he'd volunteered to come to this place and was suddenly overwhelmed. He wondered how he would find one killer amongst so many. He'd only been here a few hours and he was already bewildered. He'd set out to find a needle in a haystack.

"Here is your food, Tommy." A short dark haired woman wearing a red and white striped dress held a bowl and a spoon out to Bolam. He thanked her and took the food, a stew made with sausages. It tasted strongly of garlic, but was warm and he thought it would be filling. The woman returned shortly with some bread. "You are new here?" Her English was heavily accented.

Bolam nodded, having just taken a mouthful of hot food. The woman smiled. "Yes, just arrived today," he replied, having swallowed his food.

"Well, I hope you stay safe, Tommy. Come back again." She turned and headed off through a door. Bolam watched her go. She was attractive, not pretty like the younger girls serving from the bar, but attractive. She reminded him of a painting he'd seen in a book once. "Don't be silly, son," he said to himself, "there are other things to think about here." He shrugged, looked away then carried on eating.

He didn't stay long after he'd eaten. It had been a long exhausting journey and what he'd seen already daunted him. He did not feel like small talk. Not that there was much chance of that. There were no other officers in here and none of the gathering of soldiers had spoken to him. Caught between two worlds he thought to himself, remembering the sergeant major's speech. He made his way back to his billet. It was a grey three storey town house on the northern edge of the town, so far untouched by any warfare. Every room was occupied by several junior officers sleeping in hastily constructed wooden bunks with straw filled mattresses. The house was quiet. It seemed everyone had been equally tired. Bolam was on the top floor and he quickly climbed the bare boarded stairs before swiftly undressing and clambering into a cold bed.

# 25th April, 1915, Ypres, Belgium

Bolam woke suddenly and sat up. He looked at his watch in the dim light. He could just make out that it was half past one in the morning. Next to him and opposite, the other officers were also awake. "Did you hear that?" one said.

No one answered. Then the building shook and a noise unlike anything he'd heard before attacked Bolam's ears. Dust and small particles of plaster tumbled from the ceiling. Soot billowed out of the small fire opening at the end of the room. The noise came again. It was more than a bang, lower, but with a cracking sound at its ending. A voice penetrated the gloom. "They're shelling the railway station. Stay where you are, you'll be safe. It'll only carry on for a few minutes. They never reach this far. They shell it, we fix it. That's the way it is." Bolam recognised the voice. It was the corporal who'd led them to the billet the day before.

"Welcome to Belgium!" someone half-joked. No one laughed. Like Bolam they were all probably thinking of what the morning might bring.

What the morning brought was fog. Damp and cold. Bolam and his companions all had different destinations and each one was to be met by a guide to see them safely to their new 'homes'. Even at six in the morning

Poperinge was busy, like market day in a rural town back in England. The difference here was that instead of an industry to create food, this was a trade in the business of death.

Bolam surveyed the scene of horses and carts transporting loads: artillery, equipment, food, men and the injured. A wooden carriage pulled by two horses was laden with soldiers bandaged in various places. Most were sitting, some sporting strange grins while others were grimacing, clearly in pain. One however, looked more serious and was bandaged almost completely from head to waist and was laid out not moving. Bolam could see blood had crept through some of the bandaged layers creating dark islands against the white. This was Bolam's first glimpse of what was to come. So far his war had been sanitised by propaganda, censorship and training. He was beginning to find the real war, and it looked very different.

"Mr Bolam, sir." A smiling round faced man with a familiar accent stood in front of Bolam and saluted him. He recognised the man but couldn't place the name. "Begging your pardon, sir, Corporal Aleker, sir. Lenny Aleker, from the baker's, sir." Bolam had never been called sir so many times and the title felt strange, especially coming from someone he was acquainted with. He'd bought freshly made bread in the baker's shop on Saddler Street from Lenny on many occasions.

"Sorry, Lenny, I didn't recognise you in that uniform. How long have you been out here?" Bolam smiled, partly to put Lenny at ease but mostly because he was relieved to have a little of 'home' in the turmoil he could see before him.

"Been out here for two months now, sir, but it feels like a lot longer. Especially the last few days. Look over

59

there." He pointed at a group of men, clambering from another cart. "They're Canadians, sir, from up near St Julien, just the other side of Wipers. Hit by a gas attack yesterday, poor buggers. Some chemical called chlorine they say. The Frenchies got it a couple of days ago as well. Bloody awful thing, sir. Look at them, they can't see and can hardly breathe." He was right. The men, all with bandaging over their eyes, were being helped from a cart and lined up by a medical orderly. They could barely stand let alone walk. One collapsed directly into another and both fell spluttering and gasping. Bolam could hear them straining for breath, literally chomping at the air. "They say the only way to stop it is to piss on a bit of rag and breathe through that, sir. I don't know if it works though. Not hoping to find out, if you see what I mean."

Bolam nodded. "Let's go, Lenny," he said, "we'd better get on." And he turned to clamber into the cart Lenny had arrived in. His foot hadn't reached the step when his movement was halted midair with the sound of rifle shots; the crack of several echoed around the square. He flinched and rocked backwards then looked at Lenny who stood, head bowed and breathing deeply. A single shot rang out making Bolam jump. He'd heard about this. He looked at Lenny again and looked around the square. Through the grey of the fog he could see silhouettes of men all still, all silent, some with heads bowed, some looking towards the sky. All knew they'd just heard an execution.

"There's a firing squad post behind the town hall." Lenny looked up at Bolam. "Best make a move, sir."

Without a word, Bolam swung himself up onto the cart. Lenny placed his officer's kit bag on the back and clambered up himself. The driver flicked a whip at the horse and they set off. Bolam remembered the joker from the bedroom. Welcome to Belgium indeed.

The journey was slow going. Not only did the cart have to weave in and out of shell holes in the road every now and again, but it also had to share the space with horses and riders, motorcyclists and other forms of transport, both heading in their direction and oncoming. Bolam had imagined that this is what streets might look like in the centre of huge cities like London or Paris, but not the rural fields of Belgium. After a mile or so, the fog dissipated and it was easier to negotiate the road. The improved visibility meant that Bolam now could see the land he was riding into.

Ypres was ruined. The once magnificent medieval buildings shattered by bombing and fire. Rubble lay everywhere and to one side of what once seemed to be a huge church lay two dead horses, their sides torn open, lacerated by shrapnel. "That's what's left of the Cloth Hall, sir," Lenny said. The first words between them since leaving Poperinge. "Apparently it was beautiful until the Germans shelled the town. Imagine what they'd do to Durham if they ever got there!"

Bolam could imagine. Nothing he'd seen so far left much to the imagination at all. Nothing he'd read or heard back home had prepared him for this. The war, as far as folk in Durham were concerned, was a long way away and as much as there'd been the sporadic shelling from boats and bombing from Zeppelins in England, this destruction of a whole town was beyond comprehension.

They carried on though the town, past more devastated buildings, more smouldering piles of rubble and ruined community life. The driver stopped next to an embankment and Lenny jumped off. "This is as far as we go by cart, sir. We have to walk from here." It wasn't long before Bolam saw why. The narrow track was almost obliterated. Fields, presumably once full of neatly planted crops, were churned and pummelled into a morass of mud. Mud that seemed to stretch forever only punctuated by shining pools of stagnant water filling shell holes. Lenny stopped and pointed into the distance. "That's where we are heading, sir, Hill 60 they call it."

Bolam stared. "Hill, that's barely a rise from the level ground." He was right too, compared to the rolling hills of his home county, this was merely a mound.

"It was a little bit higher a few weeks ago but the Ozzies blew the top off with some mines. Did for the Hun they did. You should have seen the thing go up."

As they approached, Bolam could see the remains of trees standing like huge broken fingers pointing skywards. Amongst the trees there was a network of trenches, zigzagged in the style he'd learned back in Cambridge. Here though, they were not the pristine, newly dug ones he'd seen in training, these were mud ridden and waterlogged with jagged shards of corrugated iron, bits of old doors and wood scattered here and there.

They clambered down into the communications trench that led up to the trenches below the brow of the hill. Even though there were duckboards in the base of the trench, sludge squirted up and the boards rocked at every step. A frog leapt from a gap between the boards and over Bolam's boot, causing him to miss a step. "Keep your head down now, sir, we're going to be in sight of the Hun soon and there's snipers out there. Oh, and watch you don't step on one of those frogs, they'll send you arse over tit!" Bolam didn't need to be told again and he lowered his frame into an ape like walk, and kept his eyes peeled on the boards, just as the corporal was doing.

"In here, sir." Lenny leant on the side of the trench and after a gesture to follow, ducked into a tunnel. Bolam followed and disappeared into the darkness. "Keep your head down, sir, and keep watching your footing, I've stood on rats as well as frogs in here before." He heard Lenny's voice echo from somewhere ahead of him.

Feeling his way along the concrete sides, Bolam's eyes gradually became accustomed to the dark and after twenty yards or so he could just make out a glimmer of light ahead and the occasional hint of a man in front of him. After another similar stretch of tunnel, he found himself wading through water and mud before he felt the slope of the floor start upwards and eventually came to a turning that led outside into another trench. This trench was deeper than the previous one and was part of the complex he'd seen from further away. The corrugated iron strips he'd seen earlier were in fact the sides of the trench, held in place by huge iron pegs. Here and there, the same materials had been used alongside sandbags to create cover from the weather or to support the earthen roof of dugouts into the sides of the trench. He blinked to accustom his eyes to the light and was immediately aware he was being watched.

"Officer in the trench," someone announced. A dozen or so eyes stared out of filthy faces that looked as if they hadn't seen rest for days. "Welcome to Sanctuary Wood, sir." A man stepped forward, stood to attention and saluted. "Sergeant Todd, sir." Bolam looked at his platoon sergeant. Bolam guessed he was twenty-two, maybe twenty-three, but had grown a moustache to make him look older. "Sorry there are so few of us, sir, we had a bit of a night of it. The rest are further up the trench, what's left of us I mean."

"Thank you, Sergeant." Bolam looked around at the men, his men, and remembered the advice he'd been given before he left Cambridge. "The lads look like they need a rest. Why don't you let them get some food and drink and sort themselves out while you and I have a look at our orders? Give yourself a few minutes too and then we'll start."

Sergeant Todd looked slightly surprised but dismissed the men who gladly moved along the trench to find their rations and boil the kettle. The sergeant hung back. "Sir, that will mean a lot to the men. They've hardly had a wink for the last three days, what with Jerry havin' a go at the Frenchies and Canadians up the way. They've been taking pops at us and I reckon we're next."

His face looked grim and he poked his foot at the mud oozing into the trench from the side wall. "And this place doesn't make it easy. It sucks the life out of you sir. Never mind the enemy, this mud's enough to kill you. I saw a man drown in it two weeks ago. He just slipped off the pathway and disappeared. Straight down. Three of us tried to grab him. Up to my elbows I was, with Lenny Aleker hanging onto me for grim death. But we couldn't save him. He's still down there, probably forever."

"Grab yourself some food and a drink, Sergeant. Then let's see what's in store for us, eh?" Bolam could sense that these men had been run ragged and needed to feel valued. "I'll see you here in five minutes."

"Yes, sir." The sergeant saluted and turned smartly before moving further down the trench to join the rest of the men.

Bolam breathed hard, sat down on a wooden box next to the fire step and closed his eyes. It was spring. Back home the trees would be beginning to burst into life. There'd be lambs in the fields. Here, the trees were shattered, blown apart by explosives, and the animals, well they'd either been given the same treatment or eaten. Nothing lived in this land other than the rats, frogs, the lice and their human hosts. "Right, Frank, you chose this way. Remember why you're here, son," he said to himself quietly and drew another long breath. "Right, enough, time to work." Bolam shook his head and opened his eyes. Sergeant Todd was making his way back to him. Two billy cans in his hands.

"Here's a brew for you, sir." Bolam smiled and thanked him. At least things had started well with his men.

Night drew in and with it brought Bolam's first orders closer to becoming a reality. He and his platoon were to make their way to the top of Hill 60 and take stock of the German trenches below it towards Battle Wood. It was only just over a week since the mines had blown the top off the hill, taking many Germans with it. Since then, there'd been repeated attacks on the hill which had been held, but at great cost to the allied troops. Sergeant Todd had told him how he thought hundreds had been lost, including the missing men from Bolam's platoon. Fighting had been intense, hand to hand in many places, and eventually the waves of German attackers had been beaten back to their trenches. The Hill was one of the few areas of higher ground and because of that it was strategically important to both sides. Bolam's job was to assess the enemy's potential for another attack.

At exactly 8 p.m. Bolam and his men set off along the British front line trench. It was just short of a mile from the trench to the hill as the crow flies, and Bolam intended to take the shortest route. It was also a route that he thought would provide the best cover, as it had been heavily bombed and both ruined houses and shell holes were marked on his up to date map.

They made their way steadily through the trench, passing several sections with deep dugouts and tunnels. Men were cooking on makeshift braziers. Kettles were being boiled and meat fried. Most men gave them some form of greeting as they passed; a nod, a wink, a salute to Bolam occasionally. Some, sensing an element of their purpose somehow wished them luck, even in this desolate place Bolam could see that the spirit of the men had brought parts of normality into their nightmare. Their grim smiles, the thumbs up and nods showed their bond. It gave him hope.

After around twenty-five minutes, they reached the point where they needed to leave the trench and venture into the muddy wasteland everyone referred to as no man's land. It was now dark but even so, Sergeant Todd used a periscope to check for any signs of movement beyond the lip of the trench. A half-moon in a sparsely clouded night meant that there was some light

"Ready, sir?" he asked. "There's no sign of Jerry out there."

Bolam nodded and turned to his men. He could feel prickles of sweat welling up on his scalp. This was very different to any police action or the simulated fighting he'd faced in training. He realised he was scared. His men looked back at him expectantly. They'd been here before and were ready, all silent, faces, like Bolam's, smeared with mud. Knowing these men relied on him and were looking to his lead, he sucked in his courage and inched forward. "Let's go then. Good luck, lads."

As planned, two men crawled out of the trench first and eased back two deliberate breaks in the protective barbed wire to form an opening. One by one, led by Bolam, the platoon crawled out of relative safety and into the unknown. After fifty yards, Bolam stopped behind a small mound of earth and allowed the men to gather. Using only pre-agreed hand signals he gestured for them to split up. Sergeant Todd and half of the men slowly crawled off to the left, disappearing into the night, while Bolam, supported by Lenny, carried on straight ahead.

The plan was to gain two separate views of the German trenches below the summit of the tiny hill as it sloped away from Ypres. After a similar distance, Bolam felt the ground begin to rise slightly. He'd memorised the map and knew that soon they would reach the ruins of what had once been a farm. Ruins indeed. Bolam was expecting some degree of a building but nothing was left of the farm other than the remains of a few walls two to three bricks high. He hoped that his sergeant had found at least similar cover at the far end of the ruins. Once again Bolam allowed his men to regroup, ensuring no one was lost and gestured for them to gather in. He was afraid, but knew he could not show it. He looked at his men, black shapes in the darkness, and steeled himself before gesturing to move on. The land now climbed steadily and the earth beneath them was more and more churned up. Stones and other unseen objects hindered their progress as they now wove and undulated through small craters. Eventually Bolam could see they were nearing the summit and could make out the result of the blasts created by the Australians days before.

Easing himself slowly to the edge of the hill, Bolam scanned the scene. He'd imagined craters, but not like this. The ground had been devastated and crudely torn. A crater thirty feet across and just as deep stretched out before him. Beyond and to the side there were more, large and small. Against the sky, silhouettes of broken trees stood, shattered and splintered. A small pool had formed in the nearest crater and the moon's reflection smiled up at him as if it were sitting on some serene mountain lake. There was no movement. He knew Sergeant Todd should be around sixty yards to his left, edging around the top of the hill. His group had the direct route and on his signal, they followed him into the huge crater and skirted its perimeter to the other side.

Bolam surveyed the scene through the night sky. Right off into the dark of the distance nothing stirred. He could see directly down onto the enemy front line, the trench zigzagging away from him. There was no movement at all. "I need to get closer," he whispered to Lenny and signalled for the men to follow. Lenny took up the rear. On all fours initially then crawling on their stomachs they inched carefully down a slight edge to the crater, which just kept them hidden from the trench below. Soil and stones grated on Bolam's tunic, and gases released, long after being created by rotting vegetation and trapped deep below ground, teased his nostrils.

After ten minutes, they were within twenty yards of the trench. It was deeper than the British version and seemed neater somehow. A concrete pillbox, presumably with a machine gun crew inside sat menacingly to the right. Bolam steadied himself and peered carefully from his vantage point. His heart was thumping and in the silence it beat a rhythm in his ears. Still nothing. No sign of any human activity. From his new position he now had a clear view of the trench layout and eased his pencil notepad from his tunic and began carefully sketching the position and significant features. As if synchronised with his sketching, his pencil poised to portray an entrance to a dugout, a man emerged.

Bolam froze and then slowly eased his arm back to signal to his men to take extra care. Another man emerged from the dugout, followed by several more in quick succession. In the faint moonlight from his vantage point, Bolam looked down on the bobbing heads and could see the outline of helmets. Carefully and quietly, each man moved to position in the trench and to Bolam's amazement, other men, hidden in the shadows, eased out from the darkness below the lip of the trench and, as quietly as their peers, took up positions along the trench. The trench was both well manned and well organised. No signs of disarray after the recent battles. Now Bolam could see the placements of men in the trench and even in the dimness of night his eyes, now accustomed to the darkness could make out the shapes of men in the black recesses of the trench.

Silently, he began sketching again, drawing the layout and positions of where he suspected more machine guns might be situated. With the lack of light it was difficult, but there would be enough to go on when he got back to safety. Hopefully the finished jigsaw of his surveillance, together with that of Sergeant Todd, would give a fulsome picture. Bolam saw no weakness in the trench at all but equally, saw no readiness for an imminent attack.

His job finished, he signalled first and then shuffled carefully backwards away from the enemy before turning and with his men, synchronised almost as one, began crawling up the external slope towards the top of the crater, always keeping below the edge they'd followed down. With the crater lip only a yard away, Lenny, now leading, stopped abruptly and signalled to the rest with his hand. Together, they followed suit except for Bolam who, with extra care, edged forward.

"I heard a noise, sir," Lenny whispered when Bolam was near enough. "A scrape and what seemed like a voice."

Bolam tapped his chest and pointed forward, indicating that he would take a look over the ridge. He moved forwards slowly, in the process unbuckling his revolver, easing it from its holster as he silently made his way past Lenny. Crawling carefully to the edge he craned his neck to look over. His heart missed a beat then pounded. No more than six yards away, on the inside of the crater, he could see three soldiers, all wearing the unmistakably shaped helmet of the German infantry. They hadn't seen or heard Bolam and his men and were carefully crawling towards the British trench. Bolam steeled himself and edged back to his corporal, leaning in close.

"Lenny, we've got a bit of bother to deal with. Can't see any way around it. Three Germans looking like they are up to the same as us. We'll have to stop them. Let the lads know."

Lenny quickly eased back and passed the order backwards. The men quietly sucked in the cold night air and followed Lenny, who in turn followed Bolam around the outside of the crater. Bolam knew this might put them in view of the Germans below but hoped that the lack of light and roughness of the recently shredded land would keep them hidden. None of them would be seen against the skyline.

Following this line and carefully glancing over the rim every couple of yards, they tracked the Germans as they circumnavigated the inner flank of the crater and began to edge upwards. Bolam knew that he and his men needed to attack as the enemy rose to the crater rim. They would not expect an attack from the rear as all of their senses would be primed for a foe in front. He and his small group would at that point be almost parallel to the Germans, within a few yards.

Time seemed to stand still for Bolam. Only a few days ago, he had been in England. Mere months ago he had been a police officer in Durham hunting a killer he'd now followed to the trenches. Such a folly it now seemed. He remembered thinking how a killer might hide themselves in this land of death and destruction, but he'd forgotten to factor in that the hunter of such a killer was also prey to so many others. Here at the rim of a crater he was preparing to attack, and probably kill, other men. He'd never even killed an animal, let alone a fellow human being. Killing, even the chickens and pigs that were slaughtered for food, seemed alien to him and he'd avoided even witnessing these acts in his hometown. His mother had kept hens and Bolam still had vivid memories of the first slaughter he had seen. The blood seemed to run endlessly as his mother, rather than twist the bird's neck, removed its head with a large knife. To the young Bolam, the bird seemed to look at him, almost pleading, even when its severed head lay on the yard floor.

Bolam shook the bird from his mind and raised himself over the crater lip He took a couple of deep breaths to steady his nerves, aware that there was no room for error; if he missed, it would alert the Germans to their presence and the advantage of surprise would be lost. He silently cocked his revolver, aimed at the nearest man, and shot twice. Lenny was up and over at the same time and ran, rifle levelled at the men. Bolam's bullets both hit their mark and the man tumbled into the crater. His compatriots turned and while fumbling to raise their weapons, both slipped. Lenny was on one immediately, clubbing with the butt of his rifle before losing his footing too.

Bolam leaped at the third, firing at close range as his foe turned to fire his weapon almost simultaneously. The other men started over the lip themselves and two immediately helped Lenny. Bolam grappled and spun with the man towards the crater's base. They rolled together, dirt flying from their struggles, before crashing into a huge boulder. Shaken and stunned, Bolam lifted himself away from the boulder and the figure beneath him. The man's eyes were open but lifeless, blood streaming from his temple where a deep jagged wound wept. A sharp pain in his thigh snapped Bolam into focus. He could feel a wet patch on his tunic and knew that he'd been injured too, but luckily not like the sad figure below him. Bolam knew it could have been him lying there but still, here he was, a hunter of killers becoming a killer himself.

"Sir. Mr Bolam, sir." Lenny had scrambled down the slope and put his arm around Bolam's waist. "We need to go, sir, those Germans in that trench will be wondering what's going on here."

Together they clambered back to the crater's lip where the rest of the men waited. Bolam's thigh felt like it was on fire and it was all he could do not to cry out with every step. "See what we have here, sir," Lenny said. A bloodied figure was hunched between two of Bolam's men. "Put up a good fight he did, and nearly did for Nichols here." He pointed at a soldier to his right who was holding his side. "He'll be all right though an' I reckon this one," he nodded at the German soldier, "will be useful to the Brass."

Bolam remembered what the sergeant major back in Cambridge had said about leadership. "Well done lads," he said, taking time to catch the eye of each one, lingering particularly when his eyes met his injured man. "You've done a great job, now let's get back to our trench with our catch."

There was no argument and as one, they slipped over the rear of the crater and back towards relative safety, two men dragging their unconscious captive.

# 27th April, 1915, Ploegsteert, Belgium

It was dark when Bolam woke, a greyish gloom that allowed his eyes to adjust. A musty smell greeted him and added to his confusion. He could hear a soft snoring sound and other muffled noises. He stretched his arm to ease himself from his flat position and a searing pain cut into his left side. He cursed loudly and lay flat again, running his hand down his side. He was bandaged. What had happened to him? Where was he? He scanned his memory. The last thing he could remember was crawling back to the trench.

Somewhere in the distance a small light flared. "Mr Bolam." A woman's voice cut through the silence and a flickering light peeled back the darkness. As the light approached and grew stronger, Bolam could see he was in a large canvas tent. Eventually the light, a flickering hurricane lamp, was right next to him, held by a young woman dressed in white. A cross on her apron told Bolam she was a nurse. "Be steady Mr Bolam, you're safe." Her voice had the sound of the Welsh hills, almost as if she was singing to him.

"Where am I?" Bolam asked.

"This is the field hospital in Ploegsteert, you've been here for nearly a day now."

Bolam looked at her quizzically. "I don't understand. How did I get here?"

"You don't need to worry. Your injuries aren't serious. Painful, but they won't trouble you too long. Your men brought you here yesterday morning. They said you'd taken on some Germans almost single handed."

Bolam looked back at the nurse. She was pretty. Even in the dark he could see she had a warm face with smiling eyes. The events of the night in the crater came flooding back and he touched his side where he'd felt the wetness of his blood. "My injury? What..."

"A bullet wound," she cut him off. "But just through the surface of your side. You were lucky though, it could have been much worse. The doctor stitched you up incredibly neatly. Now get back to sleep, I don't want you to disturb the others."

Bolam look past her and saw that the tent contained five other beds. Her smile carried him back to his pillow and into sleep.

When he woke again, it was light. Craning his neck, he surveyed the scene before him. The tent itself was white, like the uniform of the nurse who sat at a desk near the billowing entrance flap. Clearly a replacement for the new day, this nurse seemed much older than the gentle angel who had comforted him in the dark. Including his own, furthest from the nurse, there were six beds, exactly as he'd remembered from the early hours, each one occupied by a soldier in various states of bandaging. The two lying opposite both had full facial coverings and adjacent to them there was a figure who seemed bandaged from head to foot, almost mummy-like. None moved.

Bolam slowly eased himself up from his prone position, mindful of the pain from his previous attempt.

Sucking in air and grimacing, he rode the pain and raised himself to a seated position on the side of his bed.

"Looks like you've got a Blighty wound there." A face smiled up at him from the next bed. "I'm off back today, got a bit of shrapnel in my arm. A lucky wound if you see what I mean. Got a bit of infection too so if I'm lucky I'll have about six or seven weeks at home before I come back here." Bolam managed a smile in return. "The name's Johnson, lieutenant with the Yorkshire." He extended what Bolam presumed to be his good arm out of his bed sheets and in his direction.

Bolam took the hand and shook it firmly. "Bolam. Frank. Lieutenant like yourself with the DLI, but…"

A sound from the other side of the tent, like a whimpering dog, cut their conversation. The animal-like sound came from a figure in the bed directly opposite Johnson. There were no visible features, only bandages, seemingly head to toe. Every scrap of humanity had been hidden with white, stained here and there by some form of oozing liquid.

"That's James Muir," whispered Johnson. "He's a war artist."

"Artist?" Bolam looked quizzically. "Why would you want an artist in this place?"

"Have you not seen those drawings in the newspapers? Who do you think draws them?" Johnson replied. "Apparently he was pretty good too. I'd heard he was going to be asked to draw more than for art though."

Bolam's face asked the question for him.

"Spying. You know, sneaking up on the enemy and drawing what you see. The better it is, the easier it is for the brass to understand what's going on. Doesn't look like he'll be doing that now though. Lucky if he draws breath in a few days let alone anything else. I heard the nurses talking about his kit; pencils, paints and brushes in a special bag. Under his bed apparently."

Bolam craned his neck to look. "I can…"

A sharp voice interrupted him. "Now what do you think you're doing?" There was no softness to this voice, just a rasping statement with no emotion, as starchy as the uniform on the new nurse rapidly approaching his bed. "You should not be out of bed. Let's have you back in." Before Bolam could protest, a pair of strong, rough hands grasped his ankles and hoisted his legs back onto the bed. "Now you stay there until I tell you to get out of bed." She scowled as she spoke and lent over him almost challenging him to defy her. Turning on her heels, she disappeared to her station almost as quickly as she'd arrived.

"Who the bloody hell was that?" Bolam sputtered in amazement.

His reply came not from his new companion but from the bottom of his bed. "Frank, my boy, I think you'll find that you were just bowled out by Matron."

Bolam recognised the voice instantly and looked up to see a familiar face beaming at him. "Edward, of all the places…"

"Exactly what I was thinking. What on earth are you doing out here? You're supposed to be back in my old parish solving crime."

It crossed Bolam's mind to tell his friend the whole story, but he held back when he remembered they weren't alone. "It's a long story, maybe when we have time I'll get to tell you. Never mind that though, how are you?"

"How am I? I'm not the one in the hospital bed, that's the question I'm supposed to ask."

For the next fifteen minutes Bolam explained all he could remember about his first experience in Ypres but again he found his memory empty of events after the exit from the crater. "So, with a bit of luck I'll be back with the lads soon," he finished. He could see his bedridden hospital companion looking with amazement at his words but chose to ignore him. There was no way Bolam wanted to get a Blighty wound. He had arrived in this turmoil with his own mystery filled torment and would not be put off by a wound in his side and a grumpy nurse. There was a crime to solve and he was reminded of it constantly in his dreams and moments of quietness when the victims of the murderer and their families visited him. He looked at his friend. "I need to get out of here as soon as possible."

"You've not changed Frank, but for the life of me I still have no idea why you are out here. You really should be back in Durham keeping law and order."

Bolam sidestepped the indirect question. "Never mind me, how are you?"

For a moment Bolam thought his friend hadn't heard him as he seemed distant and several seconds passed before the reply came. "Seeing you, Frank, is the first decent thing that's happened to me out here. Every day I sit by men who take their last breath. I've lost count of them. You know you can't do anything to save them, just make them feel better, at peace you know, before they go. Some of the nurses are wonderful at that too, but not all." He glanced over his shoulder at the matron. "I've heard of men thinking the nurses were their mothers in their dying moments. The nurses just pretend and hold their hand. I've even heard of one kissing a boy on his forehead and wishing him goodnight." His face darkened and he lowered his head, shaking it gently.

The shadow of doom was bluntly lifted by Matron who appeared at the foot of his bed without warning. "Mr Bolam, there's a man here to see you," she rasped and then nodded to the entrance of the tent.

A stiff figure marched in swiftly and stood to attention at the side of the matron before saluting. "Good morning, Lieutenant Bolam, sir." Sergeant Todd stood stiffly at the foot of the bed. He'd clearly made every effort to clean his uniform before his arrival. "The men wanted to make sure you were all right, sir."

"Thank you, Matron, that will be fine." Bolam prompted the nurse who seemed more than piqued at the prospect of having another person in her empire. She muttered something and skulked away. "Stand easy, Sergeant Todd, let's not worry about ceremony here. Now tell me how the men are and above all, tell me how I got here."

Sergeant Todd needed little prompting and proceeded to give Bolam chapter and verse of the events that night. It seemed he and his patrol had arrived back at the trench at the same moment as Bolam and his team. Bolam, exhausted from his struggles and his wound, had collapsed into the trench as soon as he'd reached the lip. It was only then that any of the others knew he was injured. Luckily there'd been a medical aid post only a few hundred yards away and Bolam was quickly assessed, his wound cleaned and bandaged, before being moved to his current position. He knew from his training how important this system was, not only for treating the wounded, but for ensuring men could be returned to battle fitness as quickly as possible.

"And the men? How are they?"

Sergeant Todd smiled. "Very happy, sir. It seems our little adventure gave the Brass plenty to be pleased with. That Jerry we captured must have given them what they wanted because we've all been given two days' rest. The lads are heading for Pop right now."

Bolam smiled. "That is indeed good news. Tell them I am proud of them."

"I will, sir. They'll appreciate that. They were really concerned about you though. All of them. I'm sure they'll raise a glass to you tonight." The sergeant brought himself to attention and saluted. "With your permission, sir, I'll be catching them up. I wouldn't mind a glass or two myself."

"Enjoy them, Sergeant. I'd rather be joining you but I think Matron might not approve." He glanced across to see a scowling face watching intently from the desk at the end of the tent. "What do you think, Edward?" Bolam turned to his left but found only an empty space between beds.

"Must've been called away, sir," said Todd.

After his sergeant had left, Bolam half expected to see his friend return; he thought maybe Edward had just stepped out to please the matron or to give Sergeant Todd the space and time to say what he came for. However, he didn't return and even Bolam's new acquaintance in the next bed could shed no light on how he'd slipped away unnoticed. Johnson clearly hadn't missed the conversation between Bolam and his sergeant though, "Looks like you've made a bit of impression on your men there, Bolam." He said, "I wish I could say the same. My bunch are as miserable as sin. Not at all interested in what I have to say."

Bolam kept his thoughts to himself; secretly hoping the lieutenant's wound would heal particularly quickly and put an end to his time in England.

Eight miles away, Trooper Patrick Clouting was trying to rest in the scrape hole he'd made in a corner of a trench on the front line. He'd been in the trench with others from this regiment, the Royal Irish Dragoon Guards, for three days and had been subjected to a constant barrage of trench mortars and other artillery fire from the German lines a mere three hundred yards away during the night. The explosives had destroyed the sandbagged breastworks he and his fellow soldier had fought through the mud and ooze to build that day and after three hours of emergency repairs, he was shattered. He shivered against the chilly air and moved his toes in the size eleven boots he'd chosen. Two sizes too big for him, he'd packed the toes with straw to ward off the cold. In his scrape hole, he felt safe at this point. The daytime was the time to repair and take stock as most of the shelling and exchanges between trenches took place at night. Two nights ago he'd been crawling in no man's land, repairing barbed wire which had been severed by shelling during the watch of the men who'd held the trench before he'd arrived. His uniform was still caked with the sticky mud and worse. He'd been forced to slither through the vile, polluted land, to keep under cover and out of reach of the machine gunners that repeatedly raked the area each time a German Very light flare lit up the morass of craters. It had been a dreadful task and he'd found himself crawling over body parts of soldiers from both sides of the fight, all in various forms of decay. On one occasion he'd found cover behind a long-dead German soldier, an officer it seemed. It was the epaulette he'd ripped from the dead man's uniform coat as a souvenir to show his family back home he now rolled between his gloved fingers. He was thinking of that man. His sergeant said the insignia was from a Saxon Regiment. Dead and gradually sinking into the sucking mud of these Belgian fields. Had he been a good man? Did he have a sweetheart back in Germany? Someone back home who'd never know how he'd met his death? So far, Clouting had considered himself fortunate – he'd not even had a 'lucky escape' that some men embroidered tales about. He'd been in the thick of it but at no point had a bullet whistled past his ear or had a piece of shrapnel embedded itself in his water bottle.

Reaching into his pocket, he fished out the other souvenir he'd taken from his cold companion. A medal. A cross in silver and black. It had adorned the neck of the dead officer and shone in the night as the Irishman had stared face to face into the man's rat-eaten eye sockets. He'd felt no fear himself; he was long past that after nearly six months in this hellhole. He was numb to it, numb to the inhumanity of it all and felt no malice toward the men he fought. It was kill or be killed and he was now immersed in the tragic monotony of the daily routine and each side's attrition towards the other. The German officer had been a brave man. Clouting shut his eyes and eased his head back against the mud wall, looking for sleep.

The pain that swept up the Irishman's spinal cord and fired into his brain swept his head forward, but the scream that his body emitted was stifled. The rough hand that covered his mouth, while the other twisted a bayonet deep into his spine, ensured that no sound escaped. Paralysed, Patrick Clouting could only watch with fading eyes as his killer now transferred his grip to his windpipe to squeeze his life away.

"You'll not be needing that anymore, Paddy," the killer whispered, easing the medal from the dead Irishman's fingers then slipping it into his own pocket while supporting Clouting's lifeless body against the trench wall. His right hand remained firmly clasped around the dead man's neck, keeping the body upright. Swiftly, he dropped his knees and his left shoulder, hooked his left arm between the lifeless legs and sprung up, hurling the limp body over the parapet of the trench into the morass of mud beyond. With luck, it would sink in the mire or not be discovered until sufficiently decomposed to cover up any suggestion that death didn't come from action with the enemy. A quick brush down, and the killer slipped away unseen into a nearby supply trench.

# 4<sup>th</sup> May, 1915, Ypres, Belgium

Despite Bolam's best efforts he was not allowed to leave the makeshift hospital early. Matron was as starchy as her uniform and ruled her territory with an iron fist, no matter what the rank of soldier she encountered. Bolam was no exception and it seemed she had a sixth sense that detected each and every one of his movements. There was no way he could slip out of his bed without her popping up to scold him. In the end, he gave up trying and used the seven days recuperation to gather his thoughts on his personal mission.

Lying in his bed, staring at the canvas ceiling, he had swiftly come to the conclusion that his rapid initiation into trench warfare pointed out to him that his first plan; to simply go to the battlefields and find a killer, was somewhat naive to say the least. He felt almost embarrassed at having had such a thought. How could he have been so stupid as to think that it would be so simple? The number of men and the turmoil all around meant that he needed to think differently. He realised his mission was beyond finding a killer. It wasn't just to find a man; he needed to stay alive too. His first day at the front had nearly been his last on earth and if he were to be successful, there would be no point in taking unnecessary risks. "Easier said than done," he'd said out loud late one night, causing matron to raise an eyebrow in the distance. Bolam smirked to himself and raised his own eyebrows as if in salute. "Clearly, speaking is a court martial offence."

Bolam and Lenny Aleker arrived at the billet as a storm began to throw down hail. The platoon had received orders, along with the rest of the company, to take up a reserve position to support a potential attack. The billet was in thick woods which had not yet been scarred by shelling and, according to Lenny, had been chosen to give good cover from German aircraft that had been flying aerial reconnaissance in the area. Sergeant Todd smiled as Bolam approached and saluted. "Pleased to see you, sir. You're looking much better than the last time the lads saw you. They'll be pleased to have you back, even though they would rather still be in Pop."

"I would imagine so, Sergeant Todd. Let's hope we all get a chance to get back there at some point." Bolam smiled. "I've got something to cheer the men up though," he said, untying a small petrol can from the leather bag slung over his shoulder. "Hopefully the rum will not be as bad as the water we've drunk out of one of these."

"I'm sure it won't matter, sir. As long as it's warming, it'll go down nicely."

After seeing the men were settled and the rifles were clean and in good order, Bolam made his way to the nearby tent, set up as the officers' sleeping quarters. Dismissing Lenny, he settled down to rest. As two other officers were lying in the tent and already snoring, Bolam focussed his mind back to his plan. A plan he'd hatched in the darkness of hospital tent. He needed autonomy, some way of being able to move about unimpeded by the routines of moving backwards and forwards to the front lines. If he continued as he was, ruled by orders, he would never find his man. He needed the space to investigate and to find the killer he was positive was hiding in the mayhem that was playing out in Belgium and France. His plan was risky but if he could pull it off, it might work. What he needed was to get back into no man's land.

# 5<sup>th</sup>–7<sup>th</sup> May, 1915, Ypres, Belgium

Bolam's wish was quickly granted as, while at breakfast the next morning, he received orders to take his platoon back to the front line. The battle around the small village of St Juliene had raged for days on end. Leaving the hospital, Bolam had seen the shocking results in the form of lines of casualties from gas attacks. These are the images that don't make it into the newspapers he thought. Scores of men, their eyes bandaged, a hand on the shoulder of the man in front, led by a seeing victim, were slowly and precariously weaving their pain ridden way through the communication trenches towards dressing stations. The Canadians it seemed, had suffered badly and rumours were rife that some foreign troops supporting the French had fled. Thousands of lives had been lost defending the area but, as Bolam found out, a withdrawal had been necessary. A withdrawal, which whispers amongst staff officers suggested, had cost the general his position.

Bolam had been called to divisional headquarters in Vlamertinghe to receive his orders and was met by a gloomy atmosphere. Alongside the news of the withdrawal, intelligence reports suggested that the German lines were strengthening with reinforcements, making preparations for a large-scale attack. The old line had been lost and Bolam and his men were part of the plan to hold the new one at all costs.

Bolam's men did not welcome the news but went about their preparations quickly and efficiently; most importantly they made sure their guns were cleaned and well oiled. They would need them. The mood was sombre but purposeful and without complaint. Bolam looked on with Sergeant Todd and both knew that some, if not all, of these men might never return from the line. However, it was Bolam's job to give them hope and he forced a positive demeanour into every action and every word.

The road to Ypres was now familiar to Bolam but this time he had no wheeled transport so he marched with his men to their overnight billet in Ypres. The roads teemed with people, moving to and from the ruined town, and the cratered road was even worse than Bolam had remembered. It was a constant fight to avoid carts carrying casualties coming in the opposite direction while making way for artillery being moved to the new front. Despite having passed through previously, Bolam was still shocked at the state of Ypres. Jagged spikes and shards of shattered masonry were all that was left of the once magnificent town.

It was to one of these piles of rubble that Bolam and his men were taken by the guide they had met on the edge of town, a private from the Seaforth Highlanders dressed in a khaki kilt. Bolam marvelled at the resilience of these men. He'd felt the cold in his greatcoat and trousers. How the Scots could cope with bare flesh he did not begin to comprehend.

Fallen masonry had been scraped back and piled up to fortify the entrance to the cellar of what seemed to have once been a large town house. The place smelled musty and dust rose in the gloom as they entered, "Used to be a wine cellar apparently, sir." The guide chuckled as he lit a hurricane lamp hanging from a beam in the corner of the room. "I think we're too late for any refreshments though."

Bolam smiled. No matter how dire the situation, he'd already learned that the men could find humour in anything. "Thank you, Private. We'll manage. No doubt we'll dream about it."

"A cart load of straw should arrive for you soon, sir. Now I have to move, another group to guide sir."

Indeed, not long after the guide had made his way out into the light, Bolam heard a scuffling and rattling sound above them and looked out to find two ragged looking civilians with three large bundles of straw tied to a dilapidated hand cart. Bolam wondered how these people had managed to survive. These two must have been desperate to stay on, hanging on to the remains of their former lives by tenuous threads, because the order had just recently been given to evacuate all civilians from the town immediately. He thanked the men, slipped them some coins and called to his own men to unload the cart.

Twenty minutes later the cellar looked reasonably comfortable, even though Lenny had already pointed out the variety of animal life also enjoying the warmth of the straw. "We've got our own bloody zoo down here, sir," he'd remarked sarcastically. There was no escaping the insect life that fed on the vast and replenishing buffet of human blood. The war had indeed brought them a feast. There was nothing the soldiers could do but tolerate the creatures as even attempts at removing lice and fleas with cigarettes and flames only provided temporary relief.

Bolam made the men check their guns again before resting. They would set off for the line early in the morning. Who could predict when they might sleep again?

There was little dreaming for Bolam and his men. Despite the relative cosiness of the underground bedroom, sleep came and went like the distant rumblings of artillery. Though the tattered town itself was undisturbed, the vibrations from explosions miles away reverberated through the ground and disturbed their subterranean shelter, gently chattering the brick floor beneath them. It was a long night and at five o'clock the same guide disturbed them. "Good morning, sir. I hope you slept well. I have some orders for you."

Bolam read the handwritten note and nodded to the Scot. "It says here you are to take us to Railway Wood. I assume you know the way?"

"Aye, sir, I do." His face had turned white. "It's just off the Menin Road, past Hellfire Corner."

All eyes suddenly turned to Bolam. The name was infamous and if the tales were true, the nickname was accurate. Many lives had been lost on the road at that spot. "Well, no rest for the wicked," he smirked. "Only the best jobs for us eh? You know the old saying. If you want a job doing well," he paused and looked at his men, "send a Geordie!"

The laughter broke the mood and Bolam inwardly sighed. He feared what was to come as much as the men and it had been all he could do to suck in his innermost resolve and share his courage.

The mile and a half to Hellfire Corner was slow going. As they left the ruins and ramparts of Ypres behind, the road gradually became more and more pockmarked with artillery damage, in places hastily repaired to create some form of surface suitable for horse and carts, several of which passed Bolam and his men as they made their way forward. Luckily, the early morning weather gave an initial degree of cover as a thin mist shrouded the fields either side of the road, masking it from prying eyes. The skeletal remains of larch trees, no doubt once proudly lining the road, peered eerily at them as the day became lighter and clearer.

Ahead, a strange sight greeted their eyes. Out of the dissipating mist the road ahead was lined with tattered tarpaulins, hanging from posts, tall as the sails on old fashioned galleons. "That, sir, is Hellfire Corner," the Scot explained. "We need to move fast through it. There's no cover apart from those rags and they won't stop a shell!"

There was no need for encouragement to move quickly. As one, the men doubled their pace and began catching up with two carts carrying supplies. The soldiers leading the horses were as keen as Bolam's men to get past the spot. With around twenty yards to the first tarpaulin Bolam saw a horse rear up, twisting against the weight of the cart. Seconds later a shell exploded directly in front of it, lifting both horse and cart into the air and throwing the driver backwards to the ground.

Bolam lost no time and screamed at his men. They followed him, first running, then throwing themselves to roll over the slight edge of the road amongst the churned up rubble and mud to gain some cover from the now developing barrage of artillery fire. Shell after deafening shell pounded the road for several minutes before the guns fell silent. The air was thick with dust and a smell that Bolam instantly recognised. Years earlier, as a teenager he'd visited a nearby farm when pigs were being slaughtered. The sickly metallic smell that drowned the air then, he smelled again and tasted it as if it coated his tongue and lined his nose. But that wasn't the only thing that made his flesh crawl. The screaming. The screams came not from humans but from horses. Shrieks, piercing and terrible, shredded the air.

Bolam craned his head, along with several of his men, and surveyed the carnage on the road. Three horses lay directly in front of them, their bodies cut open by shrapnel, and ahead, the unlucky beast Bolam had first seen startled lay on its back on top of the cart it had once pulled. Foam frothed from its mouth and it writhed in pain, twisting against the harness, now like a spider's web, trapping it. One of its back legs flailed limply, clearly dislocated.

Without warning a rifle shot rang out and the horse fell still. Bolam looked across the road and saw the source of the shot. The horse's driver, himself bloodied, had somehow survived, probably as his animal had taken most of the force of the explosion, and had ended the beast's suffering with his rifle. Ahead, a second horse was dispatched by another shot and the screaming stopped. The road fell eerily silent as Bolam and his men, all unscathed, looked on with disbelief.

A voice brought Bolam back to reality. "Sir, we need to move. If the air clears, they'll see us and let rip again." It was the Scot. His face covered in dust. "This way."

Bolam and his men peeled away from their cover onto the edge of the road and followed. They crawled past the scene of shattered carriages and horses, doing their best to avoid the blood-soaked earth and horseflesh spread across the road. Their drop off point was just past the tarpaulins, now even more ragged. One by one they followed the Scot down a short drop from the road to the ruined railway line, running to their destination.

The line ran towards the north east away from the road and ahead, around 750 yards away, Bolam could make out a wood through the clearing mist. It took a further hour of scrambling and crawling, making use of every aspect of cover they could find, to reach their destination. The wood, presumably once a splendid gathering of trees, was, on close inspection neither splendid nor alive. The trees, which at this time of year should have been well into their spring awakening, were long since incapable of waking after a winter slumber. Bolam though, was grateful for the cover and the brown gnarled bodies of dead oaks provided shelter.

"I'll leave you here, sir." Bolam smiled at the Scot, knowing he had to risk his life once again returning to Ypres.

"Good luck, Private," Bolam said. There was no time for sentimentality even though he knew what was in store for his guide. He now had to turn his thoughts to his men and their orders. They were to defend this wood and there would be no retreat.

The wood near Bolam was full of soldiers digging. It was clear that a series of new trenches was being established for the defence of the area. It didn't take long before Bolam found who he was looking for. Captain Wallace of the King's Shropshire Light Infantry was a wiry man with a thin blond moustache which, contrary to his aim, made him look young compared to Bolam. Oddly, it was expected that officers grew a moustache and Bolam had grown one despite his own personal taste. However, Wallace was anything but immature and within minutes he'd allocated Bolam and his men a section of land at the north western corner of the wood to establish their 'living quarters'.

It was another six hours before the trench was in a state to be occupied, with only rudimentary scrape holes in the sides for the men to curl into and sleep in. It was in that position that Bolam retired to after establishing a watch rota and checking all men had clean guns and would be ready for action in the event of an attack.

# 8th May, 1915, Ypres, Belgium

The first shell landed at 5.30 a.m., shattering both the silence and the large stump of an ancient oak twenty-five yards from Bolam's trench, sending shards of wood flying over the top of the trench. The world around Bolam seemed to erupt. Shells poured into the wood and to his left he could see further down the line the bombardment stretching into the distance. This was it, he thought to himself. This was the assault they'd been expecting. He knew from his training and from accounts given by his peers that the ground attack would follow the shelling. There was nothing to be done other than to wait and hide, hoping the shells would not seek him and his men out.

The bombardment continued, shell after shell, shattering trees, throwing up plumes of earth. From his scrape hole, Bolam saw a shell burst right on the lip of the trench, not twelve feet away, shattering sand bags and hurling corrugated iron in all directions as if it were paper. Somewhere near there were men, like him, just hoping they'd see it through and he knew and he was helpless to protect them. There was no better cover. They were stuck in a roulette game with shells instead of balls deciding their fate. If lady luck was with them, the German gunners' aim would not be true today and life would prevail.

After what seemed like days, the wood fell silent. Bolam rolled into the trench and shook off the dirt that had built up over him. He needed to get his men ready for the assault he expected next, so began making his way down the trench. Men were extracting themselves and comrades from the dirt that had rained over them and, at the point where he'd seen the trench lip shatter, Sergeant Todd and two others were digging furiously. An arm emerged and quickly the rest of the body attached to it followed. Lenny Aleker's lifeless face, blue from suffocation, flopped forward.

Bolam swallowed hard and moved forward. Taking Lenny's broken body, he laid him to one side of the trench and breathed hard, staring at his face. The reliable smile had gone forever. He paused, taking a last look at the baker from Durham, briefly picturing him back home wearing his apron behind the counter, before snapping back to the present. "Lads, they'll be coming soon. We need to be ready."

There was no need to say more. Training kicked in. Every man knew his position and role and within minutes the fire step was occupied. Right down the line Bolam could hear orders being issued, words of encouragement and oaths being sworn. And Bolam's soul shook.

It was not the attack Bolam had expected. A more sinister enemy came first. The cry he'd hoped never to hear made his flesh crawl. "Gas! Gas!" Bolam immediately reached into his right breast pocket and removed a thick pad of gauze. The whole battalion had been issued with these pads after the first gas attack. He could see men around him doing the same; a look of panic filled the eyes of the man next to him.

"You'll be all right, Sam," Bolam said calmly, "just stay high. Remember it sinks down low in the trench." He whisked the top off his water bottle and doused the gauze, tied it across his mouth and nose with string and peered down the trench.

Even with the gauze he smelled it before there was any in sight. A pungent acrid odour that seemed to bite at his throat. Then he saw it. A yellowish green haze at first, then a fog, far off to his right down the line, like a wave emerging from the broken trees before it fell over the lip of the trench and sank down, cascading like a putrid waterfall. It was mesmerising, almost pretty. A bewitching spectacle, but a deadly one. The breeze brought it towards them. Down the line he could see men panicking, covering their eyes. Some left the trench, throwing themselves onto the higher ground. Bolam expected gunfire but none came. The gas would have to clear before the Germans could attack. They wouldn't risk their own troops in this and there was no open ground for machine gunners or snipers.

"Quick lads," Bolam called. "Get out of the trench. Climb a tree if you can." He hauled himself up and over the parapet, rolling into no man's land. It was only three days ago he'd wished this upon himself but now he regretted those thoughts. There was a tree stump only ten feet away and without further thought he hauled himself onto it. The wave of yellow slowly approached and lapped around his feet. He could see another man's hands clinging to the trunk of a thinner tree and guessed the rest of his body was pressed against the other side, possibly standing on the stump of a branch or with his feet wedged into a hollow at the other side. Below and towards the trench, another man stood leaning against a tree, almost submerged in the rolling gas, hands over his eyes, face pointing upwards. Screams and cries now replaced the sound of high explosives in the wood.

It took all of Bolam's resolve not to panic himself, but to wait until the tidal flow of the gas dispersed. It was gunfire that spurred him to clamber down into the dissipating smog. The ground attack was underway.

The trench stank of chlorine gas but not enough now to hinder anyone. Several of the men had not managed to beat the gas and were struggling to breathe, gasping and hacking as their lungs burned and eyes watered profusely. Bolam had no time to provide aid and instead rallied the remaining able-bodied men.

Sergeant Todd appeared, clutching a hessian bag divided into pouches. "You seen one of these before, sir?" he asked, pulling a grooved, metallic, oval shaped object from one of the pouches. "Mills Bombs. New out here, apparently designed by a bloke in Sunderland of all places! I saw some being unloaded in Pop. You pull this pin and throw it." He handed three to Bolam and draped the bag over his shoulders. "They might come in handy."

In their section of trench, there were now only nine men fully fit to fight. They lined up grimly as the gunfire drew closer, eyes straining into the wood, bayonets fixed. Bolam held a Lee Enfield rifle, borrowed from a gas casualty. His officer's pistol would be less accurate firing in this woodland.

The first glimpse of the enemy in the trees caused a firestorm from both sides. Bolam and his men fired over the lip of the trench at the emerging, grey-uniformed, foe. They advanced and dropped like stones as the rifles picked them off. More and more approached, undeterred by the accuracy of the British riflemen. Sergeant Todd stepped down from the fire step and screamed, "Heads down, lads!" He pulled the pin of a Mills Bomb before hurling it like a cricket ball in the direction of the approaching Germans. The explosion was deafening and Bolam felt shrapnel and dirt whizz over his head.

Three more grenades were thrown, then Bolam and his men peered over the trench lip. A German struggled to gain his footing and was immediately picked off by at least two shots. For a second or two Bolam thought the attack had been halted, then more came, rushing this time. Two more bombs from Sergeant Todd cut into their attackers again, but before he could throw once more, a German soldier appeared on the lip of the trench. His shot caught the sergeant in the chest and spun him sideward. Bolam reacted quickly and, before the German could reload, grabbed his legs and toppled him into the trench. Bolam was on him as soon as he hit the trench floor, ramming the rifle butt into the man's face.

The attack continued with wave after wave of enemy soldiers emerging from the trees. British gunfire and Mills Bombs cut them apart but still they came, grinding into the defences remorselessly. Bolam looked left and right. He was on his own now in his section of trench, the rest of the men now, like Sergeant Todd, either dead or wounded. More Germans were advancing and the defence was dwindling. Bolam was resigned to this being his last stand and loaded his rifle.

In that instant a hand grabbed at his ankles, another pulled at his waist and he toppled backwards, his fingers slipping from the rifle. It was the German he'd hit earlier, face bloodied and twisted with pain. Bolam once again landed on top of the man, the force of his impact knocked the wind out of his assailant causing him to convulse.

Bolam pushed himself up on his knees away from the German and grappled with the edge of the trench, fingernails scraping and splitting as they sought for purchase. His rifle had wedged itself upright against the trench wall and Bolam grasped it, using it as a prop to raise himself. Chaos continued all around, the noise of rifle fire, men screaming, cursing and crying with pain all blended into an almost jungle-like cacophony of sound.

"Get your head down, sir!" Bolam just made out the direction of the voice and looked to his left. Sergeant Todd, blood streaming from his chest, slumped against the trench wall, had a Mills bomb in his hand and was preparing to throw it. Once again Bolam dropped to the trench floor and watched as the sergeant pulled the grenade's pin and with huge effort, pain clearly coursing through his shoulder, drew back his arm to send it flying toward the attack. The throw never came. Sergeant Todd's head jerked back violently as a bullet took him mid-forehead.

Time seemed to stutter. Bolam strained to see where the shot had come from and caught sight of a grey figure standing on the lip of the trench, twenty yards distant. Closer to him, the hand his sergeant had raised dropped like a hammer and the grenade, pin missing, rolled free. Simultaneously, the grey figure stooped to clamber into the trench. Bolam reacted quickly, pulling himself forward, using the German he'd fought with for leverage and flattened himself into the mud.

The explosion, despite all of the other noise, was deafening and the air hot. Stones, metal, dirt and flesh flew in all directions. Then silence fell.

It was almost dark when Bolam opened his eyes. He coughed and blinked to clear his vision; there was the light tinge of chlorine still corrupting the air and the foul gas stung his throat and eyes. His head ached and his ears were ringing but other than that he could feel no pain or sense an injury. However, something near him brought his mind to focus. There was no sound, but he felt movement near his feet. He kept still. Breathing slowly. His right cheek pressed into the mud. In his mind, he played back the last events he could remember. The advance of the Germans, the fight, Sergeant Todd being shot. Shot again. The Mills Bomb! The realisation of what had happened shocked Bolam into readiness. Who was moving near him? Not Todd, that was certain. The only two other candidates were German; Todd's killer and the Hun he'd fought. Bolam pondered his options. The movement was still there, erratic, but definite movements. Had one of the Germans survived the blast too? He'd have to find out. There was no choice.

Summoning all his strength, Bolan twisted free from the sucking mud, his head thumping, and sat upright, bracing himself for an attack. None came. There was no one, not that he could see far. Even so, he again felt movement near his feet, as if someone was moving the area of earth around him. This time though his eyes shot to the place where he felt the vibration. A rat. He'd seen plenty before but not like this, nor so close. Ignoring him, plainly without fear, it tugged at what Bolam could see was human flesh, part of a hand. It pulled at the flesh, causing the fingers to twitch in a surreal manner. Repulsed, Bolam looked for a weapon and found the scattered butt of what he presumed was the rifle he'd picked up earlier. He caught the beast with a looping swing, sending it skittering across the trench floor. It sat up, regained its composure and looked back defiantly at

Bolam. It took three handfuls of stones and earth to frighten the creature enough to see it disappear behind a shattered tree stump.

Bolam eased himself into a more comfortable position. He could see no immediate danger. The German he'd grappled with was dead now, if he hadn't already been. Bolam could see, even in the increasing darkness that he'd being partly shielded from the blast by the man. A man. Just like him. It could have been him. The grim face of the German, bloodied from the blows Bolam had made, lay before him, his tunic ripped apart.

A white piece of paper poked out of the rags. Bolam carefully reached over and gently plucked the paper from its owner. It was a letter, folded into four. As Bolam unfurled it, it was clear it had been opened and refolded many times. The creases were ragged. Spidery dark writing covered the page. Bolam could neither speak nor read German but this was clearly a letter from a mother to a son. He could make out a name, written formally at the top of the letter adjacent to the address. Looking back at the dead German, Bolam stared silently for a while then whispered, "Heindich Kaningasser, I will make sure your mother knows you were a brave man." With that, he folded the letter and slipped it into his own pocket. "Before I do that though," he continued, "I need to disappear."

# 10th May, 1915, Ploegsteert, Belgium

It took Bolam two hours to crawl and scurry away from Railway Wood and a further two days of walking, hiding and sleeping rough to get back to the dressing station. It was a huge emotional challenge. He knew he was leaving the scene of the fight. He had no idea of the fate of his men, though he suspected the worst. His duty as an officer was to check on them, report back to headquarters and to take on further orders. All this he knew and yet he wrenched himself away, effectively deserting his post and making himself a traitor to his country.

Since his days behind the lines staring at the ceiling of a hospital tent, he'd fought battles in his mind over what was right and wrong in his plan. Every time he found an answer and agreed with himself that he should go ahead, another nagging doubt sprung back at him. There, in the dirt of a blood soaked battleground he made the decision. It was now or never. If he was to find the killer, he had to act. No matter what the consequences. If it went badly… well, he didn't think it was worth dwelling on.

He'd avoided everyone as he made his way across country. Once away from the wood he'd kept low, crawling between ditches, small craters and shattered buildings. He'd settled at the end of his first night as a deserter in the ruins of a barn. The roof had collapsed but there was enough of a space to crawl in and shelter from the cold and light rain. It was unlikely, he thought that he'd be found in such a place. He ate the small amount of rations he had with him and sipped from his water flask, knowing he had to keep some until he found a source of drinkable water. Despite the situation, he was rather pleased with himself, although nervous about his plan. He hoped he'd be listed as 'missing in action', though this status itself caused him grief. What would this do to his family if they were told? Once again wrestling with his conscience, Bolam drifted off into a fitful sleep, punctuated by sporadic artillery fire in the distance.

He'd followed the same routine in the dark of the next night and gradually made his way under the cover of darkness towards Ploegsteert. In the last hour, he'd managed to find some rest in a storage hut, about two hundred yards from the tent in which he'd recently recovered in. He stayed there, tucked in a corner behind a stack of wooden boxes, not sleeping and waiting for darkness to fall. He'd almost been spotted earlier. A nurse had entered the hut and rummaged noisily for something before giving up her search, swearing and slamming the door behind her. Bolam had pressed himself to the shadowy wall and tried to silence his breathing. Only when she left did he move, sighing with relief. Since then he'd squeezed behind a large wooden box, listening to every sound, watching through the cracks at the dimming light outside.

He looked at his watch and through the wall of the hut. It should be dark enough now, he thought, and eased out of his hiding place. Instinctively he was careful not to catch his holster on the boxes and quickly remembered he'd lost his revolver in the fight two days earlier.

Silently, concentrating on every footstep and with total focus on listening for sounds that might indicate a presence nearby, he edged towards the door. He had no real escape plan should he be disturbed, but had thought he might simply collapse on the floor and explain something believable later. After all, he could plead concussion.

The door creaked a little as it opened and Bolam saw it was raining. Light drizzle, which added to the darkness, made visibility very poor. "Perfect," he murmured and stepped out cautiously onto the duckboard. After carefully closing the door, he made for the tent that for a few days he'd known as home. He'd decided there was no point at this stage in sneaking about; that would come next. He just needed to brazenly stride out. There were no guards inside the perimeter of the dressing station, it wasn't a strategic site and far more important places needed protection of that sort. It took just over a minute to cover the ground to the tent and as he drew closer he could see a faint glow within, casting shadows against the canvas. This was exactly what he had hoped for.

He stepped off the duckboard and into the mud. There were still trees left in this area and he made for them, just to the right of the tent. He could now count the beds comfortably, using the shadows as a guide. He knew his bed had been on the side of the tent he was looking at and, counting from the entrance, he deduced that he had occupied the ninth one. That meant his target was number eight on the opposite side.

Bolam stayed in the shadows and edged around the tent. Luckily the trees extended past it and he could use a similar vantage point to select his target. It took only seconds. From this point he could not go back. If he was caught now, it would be hard to explain, no matter how passionate he was about catching a murderer. The seeds had been sown in this field hospital and the plan developed in the cellar in Ypres. Miraculously, James Muir had survived. Despite multiple wounds he had clung on to life and still lay in the bed opposite Johnson as he was when Bolam left the field hospital. The whimpering had stopped and was replaced by an occasional moan or a gargling sound, one of the nurses explained that this was as a result of the burns he'd suffered inside his throat.

The artist, apparently resting in a dilapidated barn, not dissimilar to Bolam's recent cover, found his accommodation hit by German shellfire and was crushed by falling masonry. The straw around him had ignited from the explosion and the resulting hot air had almost asphyxiated Muir. Luckily another soldier had just stepped out to relieve himself and managed to drag the officer from the rubble.

Bolam wanted his kit. It was going to be part of his life insurance; his cover story. He'd seen the artist's bag and other possessions every day when he was in this tent and now he was there to make them his own. In fact, Bolam wanted more than the man's things, he wanted his identity.

Keeping his eyes fixed on the spot he'd pinpointed, Bolam moved silently forward to the tent. It was fixed with large wooden pegs on both guy ropes and around the base. Additional strength was given with wooden staves every four feet. This helped Bolam as he could latch his eyes to the particular gap between the staves he needed. He quickly went to work loosening an opening at the base of the canvas. Even though the ground was soft it was slow and tense work. He was more exposed here. Gradually the earth gave up its grip and the peg came free. Five minutes later and he'd released a second peg. The canvas was now loose enough for him to crawl under.

Easing the canvas up, he took a last look around him and pressed his head through the gap. Perfect. He was in the exact spot he'd calculated and was emerging right behind the bed, totally out of sight of the matron or any wandering nurse. The floor of the tent had been boarded and he gradually raised his chest over the lip and his head under the bed. His eyed gradually adjusted and the underside of the bed became clear. Nothing. It was empty. No bag, no possessions, nothing but dust and a piece of lint. The artist was gone. Bolam held his breath to prevent himself from cursing out loud. What now? His thoughts swirled. He had no second plan. This was it. He'd have to go back to headquarters and...

"Sir, this is Sister Williams, she's in charge tonight." A deep voice shattered the silence.

Bolam froze.

The voice that replied crackled and flowed with a confidence Bolam hadn't heard before. "Well Sister, take me to the artist. I need to see him urgently. Snap to it."

Three pairs of feet clicked and clattered past Bolam's hiding place and from his dusty spot he followed the light shimmering from the nurse's hurricane lamp as it shone on the floor and moved down the tent to a bed two places further on. Bolam craned his neck as far as he dared to see this visitor who wanted so desperately to see the injured officer. As the speaker's face partially came into view, Bolam almost gasped in astonishment, but held his breath for a second time.

The man who had once been First Lord of the Admiralty stood only four yards from him. Bolam had read about him in the papers, notably the criticism he had come in for over his involvement in a house siege and the disaster in the Dardanelles. Bolam knew the man had lost his post after the latter incident but nevertheless, he was still shocked and amazed to see Winston Churchill in this small tent in Ploegsteert.

"This is Lieutenant Muir, sir." The nurse's soft voice contrasted sharply with Churchill's. "As you can see, he's in a bad way."

"Can he hear us?" Churchill replied.

"We don't think so, sir. His facial injuries are extensive; his ears were burnt off and the doctor thinks that there's internal damage from the heat and explosion as well."

"And will he survive?"

Through the light Bolam could just see the nurse's face, partly lit by her lamp. Her face dropped. "No more than a few days, sir." Her voice caught. "We don't even know if he can feel anything. He doesn't move and we can't feed him. We've managed to get some water into his mouth, but most of it just pours back out. He's stopped making any sounds now other than when his breathing is laboured"

"I see." Churchill turned to the officer with him. "His family will be shattered. Their only son you know. Friends of my mother. I'll prepare my letter. Keep me informed."

It was all very matter of fact. At least that was how it appeared to Bolam. Yet here was a man whose decisions had cost many lives and according to the papers, a man who wore the guilt heavily. Maybe that's just how you had to be when you dealt with matters of such huge importance, Bolam wondered? He hoped he'd never have such a responsibility.

The footsteps clattered again and jerked Bolam back from his thoughts. He watched the light pass and waited until the room was still, then eased backwards through the canvas. As before, it was easy to pinpoint the right spot and within a minute he'd managed to ease himself to the underside of the artist's bed. The bag was there, towards the end of the bed. Slowly and silently, Bolam pulled himself forward, ploughing a line through the dust until he could reach the handle of the bag. He began drawing it towards him. The dust seemed to help it slide easily and he shuffled quietly backwards, easing the bag with him in rhythm with each move. His technique worked well and he managed to get the bag back to the head of the bed before it caught on a gap in the floorboards, causing his hand to twitch up against the bed base. The wire frame pinged like a guitar string, resonating down the tent. Again Bolam froze. A light moved down the tent once more, accompanied by footsteps.

Bolam knew this was a make or break point. He'd crossed the line now and, if caught, the punishment would not be gentle. His heart thumped and the blood pounded in his head as he saw in his thin strip of vision available to him, the nurse's feet and swishing skirt moving purposefully to the centre of the tent, only a few feet away. He imagined the nurse rotating the lamp like a lighthouse as she studied her patients. Minutes passed before the nurse seemed satisfied that all was well and clicked her way back to the end of the tent. Bolam held still for a further five minutes before he moved again and succeeded in extricating himself and his prize from the tent.

He looked at the bag; despite the shadows, he could make out its shape. It was essentially a leather doctor's bag with added straps to allow it to be carried on the shoulders. Bolam knew it held his immediate destiny. After one last look around, he hoisted the bag onto his back and left. He would take on the identity of a war artist now and like many of the others in that 'trade' he would be a spy. Except he would be spying on his own side.

Five miles to the east of Bolam another bag was the centre of attention. Externally it was almost identical in design to the artist's, but without the shoulder straps. Inside, however, was a different matter. Worn hands raised a string necklace from around the owner's neck. A key hung free of its hiding place and glinted like the eyes that now admired it. Nimble fingers grasped it, quickly released the bag's lock, flicked the twin catches open and prized the sides of the bag apart. Light from a single candle on a shelf illuminated the contents. No paints, brushes or pencils in here. The contents of this bag shone and scattered the flickering light.

The face that beamed down into the bag glowed not just with the yellow light, but also with pride in the collection. Each side of the bag opened to reveal a series of cantilevered shelves. Each shelf was divided into small compartments, and in most of these lay a shining gathering of treasures. Buttons, badges, medals; all polished and held in place with white cotton. Each had its own place, seated in luxury. None were duplicated. All, proudly and carefully stored, as a scientist might take care of the most fragile of ancient fossil specimens.

The same nimble fingers reached into a pocket, removed a small parcel of dark cloth and from it turned out a black cross onto a pale palm. Keen eyes studied the item. A perfect form with two lines of symmetry. Black enamel surrounded by polished metal. The Iron Cross, First Class. It had long been a goal of the collector to own one. He knew they were highly prized by their owners. Even so, he had been quite surprised how the injured German on the stretcher had struggled to keep it as the collector began to remove it from the left lapel of his jacket. In the end though, a hand over his mouth and nose had sapped the life out of him and the medal had been won.

Carefully, the medal was placed into a central compartment; its blackness contrasting starkly with its white cushioning. The collector sighed, smiled and locked the bag before tucking it away behind a loosened plank in the dugout. From his pocket he took out a small, black book and flicked it open to a page where the corner had been folded down. His finger worked down the text, stopping at a line that had been well thumbed and read out loud, "'The slothful man roasteth not that which he took in hunting: but the substance of a diligent man is precious.'" Looking back at the plank he smiled again. "Oh yes, Lord, I am indeed diligent and the fruits of my hard work are truly precious. My work will continue. I will never slacken. I will not stop. Nothing will interrupt my toil." He flipped the bible shut and looked to the boarded ceiling, lost in thought, while in the distance the rumble of artillery cracked the night.

# 26<sup>th</sup> May, 1915, Boesinghe. About Two Kilometres North of Ypres

Bolam sat in total darkness. It was a habit he'd developed over the last two weeks. The nights were getting lighter but Bolam was unusual in wishing they weren't. Since leaving Ploegsteert, he'd adopted a new identity. While he still carried the leather identification tags around his neck that marked him as James Bolam, externally, he was now a war artist with a new name and a new look.

Inside James Muir's bag he'd found a document, written on card, which identified the artist and explained that the bearer of the card had the freedom to roam the battlefields and surrounding area without interference or hindrance. The only exception would be if a higher ranking officer knew there was to be severe and imminent danger or that the artist could compromise any planned action. Bolam had used the artist's own pen and ink to skilfully alter the name on the card. James Muir became Jameson Murray.

Until this point Bolam had, rather reluctantly, sported a thin and closely trimmed moustache, as was the expected custom for officers. Now, however, he'd allowed his facial hair to sprout, and his upper lip was now covered with a dark thatch, which he intended to grow into a bushy walrus-like affair. His final facial amendment was a pair of round spectacles he had discovered in the artist's bag. Luckily, the lenses weren't too thick, and Bolam could manage well enough with them if he needed to. The finishing touch, which Bolam was particularly proud of, was to administer several carefully chosen accidental daubs of oil paint on his trousers and jacket.

None of this disguise had been put to the test though, as so far he'd moved only at night under the cover of darkness, gradually finding his way across country and through Ypres to his present position; a cellar under a ruined house in Boesinghe. Like all the villages in the area, this one had been flattened by artillery fire, but after several nights sleeping rough, Bolam had gradually gained more and more expertise at seeking out shelter.

On his travels he heard the sounds of battle, saw the flashes from explosions and felt the pangs of guilt for walking away. He wasn't a coward. He knew that. But if he were to be caught, that would not be the impression a court-martial would be given. This was when he again realised that by not returning, he'd be reported as being missing in action and it was likely that his mother and sister would receive the news soon after. He hadn't totally considered this. What had he done? Would they ever be able to forgive him… if he survived? Still, there was no turning back. He'd locked himself into a path and he had no idea where and when it might end.

The time on his own gave him thinking time. He'd set off to war to carry out a task and this was the first real opportunity he'd had to think properly about it. How stupid he'd been. The principle was right. Nothing would convince him that the killer wasn't out here. He just hadn't realised the enormity of the task. The killer could be anywhere. Bolam had just hoped that Belgium was the right place as he'd been sent here alongside soldiers from many other northern regiments. But there was still a huge chance his quarry could be in France, Italy or even further afield, such was the spread of the war. Not only that, he hadn't thought at all about the possibility of his man being killed. He'd come close himself – more than once – and if that happened to his killer, he'd never know who it was he sought. As much as Bolam wanted his man, he wanted him alive. He wanted him to face trial and then be hanged for his crimes. For there to be satisfaction for the families of his victims, especially Mrs Bell; they needed their four penneth of flesh and a corpse in a muddy field in Flanders wasn't going to give them that.

In his dark hiding places each night, Bolam's plan began to evolve. He began by turning the investigation and clues over and over in his mind, trying to reacquaint himself with the case. He was sure of the motive. This was a man who liked shiny objects and liked to kill. There was no accident in the killing. Anyone could have acquired such objects by theft or other skulduggery. No, thought Bolam, this man liked the kill. He'd come across men like this before. Not killing humans though. Men who professed to be hunters, but actually simply enjoyed the killing of animals for fun. He'd seen them laugh and watch with glee when a rabbit not properly dispatched was writhing in pain, before letting the dogs tear it apart. He would have liked to see the same men in the trenches out here, where the 'rabbits' have guns of their own.

It was that last thought that formed the backbone to Bolam's theory. This was not likely to be a fighting man. Oh no, he thought, this man will avoid the front line when he can. In his mind's eye, he'd begun listing the possible jobs and places he might begin his search. Most front line

114

soldiers did other jobs when away from the sharp end. They did a whole variety of jobs and tasks from carrying water to delivering rations, but Bolam didn't think his man would be amongst them because of the simple fact that they were always required to have a stint in front of enemy guns. The Artillery perhaps? No, the Germans shot back. Driver? A possibility, but not if it involved anything being taken to the front. Miners? He could be a miner. There were plenty from Durham who could dig, but he'd heard that the Germans mined too and if they met underground or one side discovered the other digging, it was often disastrous. So that was only a possibility. The list went on until one stood out.

# 27<sup>th</sup> May, 1915, Boesinghe. About Two Kilometres North of Ypres

The guns had fallen silent over the last few nights. Bolam wasn't to know it but in his absence, the battle had ground to a halt after weeks of attrition. He woke and prepared to start his new role as a war artist. After eating the now stale bread, he'd stolen two nights ago from a cart left unwatched by a soldier relieving himself nearby, Bolam climbed out of the cellar.

It was not by accident that he'd ended up in this area of Ypres. There were several field hospitals and dressing stations dotted around and Bolam's pondering had brought him to the conclusion that men working in these places were the least likely to be called go over the top. He simply didn't imagine a doctor would be the person he sought but he knew there were other roles in field hospitals covered by men. Of these, he thought stretcher-bearers were less likely as they often bravely picked up casualties from the field of battle and had been known to become targets for snipers. But he couldn't rule them out as he thought it wouldn't be impossible to avoid that part of the job by always ensuring they were quick off the mark and picked up the casualties already back to their own lines.

Bolam's plan was to use the rough map of the Ypres Salient he found in amongst the artist's belongings to visit as many field hospitals as possible in his adopted role. It may well have been a plan the artist himself had had, because along with trenches, various fortifications and significant buildings (or what was probably left of them) there were many different sized crosses he believed signified a medical installation of some form. He'd won a prize at school for art but this was a far cry from those days. He hadn't drawn or painted since his school days and it was not like this then. The nearest he'd come to observational drawing was a vase of flowers his teacher had set up in the middle of the room for the class to draw. Somehow, Bolam didn't imagine there'd be many flowers around.

Over the last few days, he'd experimented with Muir's tools of the trade. He'd found two books of bound paper in the bag, one containing several sketches made by the artist. Bolam was impressed. Though only sketches, using a soft pencil, Muir had managed to convey the slump-shouldered exhaustion of those returning from the front line, trudging with mud-laden boots along dirt tracks, blank gazes concealing the horrors they'd witnessed. A few strong, deft strokes depicted the charred remains of trees peppering the bleak landscape and the desolate morasses of mud. Muir had captured the mood of men, the shattered ruins of Ypres and its surrounding landscape brilliantly.

There was little chance of Bolam maintaining those standards but as he thought and pondered how he might fit the role, he decided he needed a tactic that allowed him to draw without being compared to 'proper' artists, and in a manner that could help him in his search.

So it was a very nervous Bolam who set off down a road parallel with the canal heading to Ypres. Like all other roads in the area, its surface was ruined and littered with reminders of the war. Bits of metal, masonry, shattered wood and other bits and pieces of debris, often in the road, but mostly moved to either side to allow movement. There was a business-like buzz about the place. Men, civilian and military, walked and marched, leading horses or mules pulling carts or carrying boxes of ammunition and supplies. In the air, two aeroplanes buzzed. Bolam marvelled at their height. They were so high he couldn't see the men who flew them. Were they ours? he wondered. What were they doing up there? He'd heard these machines were being used to spy on the enemy from above and that the enemy was doing the same. Although he'd never witnessed it, there were rumours there had been fights in the sky between the two sides with the pilots taking up their revolvers to shoot at each other. He tapped his holster, the revolver he'd found in the artist's bag had filled an empty gap. What next, he wondered, how many other ways would men dream up of killing one another?

It took Bolam around an hour to weave his way through to what he believed on the map was a small field hospital near the edge of the canal. The high dyke offered protection from gunfire and he could see several thick concrete structures had been built to make the task of saving lives as protected as possible. Several small tents clung to the sides of the structures and to the right, a gathering of wooden crosses of differing designs, all white, contrasted sharply with the tall gangling remains of trees standing guard on the top of the dyke. In the far right corner, three men toiled with spades. Clearly another soldier whose luck had deserted him was to be buried there.

Further away in the direction of Ypres, still under the shield of the dyke, there seemed to be a gathering of dark tents and soldiers purposefully milled here and there around them. A regimental base, he guessed; somewhere to steer clear of. He needed to keep his contacts purposeful and to avoid the possibility of getting sucked into any conversation that might unveil him as an impostor.

Bolam walked towards the field hospital. This was totally unlike the one he'd spent time in. Clearly, this was not a place for the wounded, but a place where men died or received life-saving treatment before being shipped out, away from the front. A dressing station, not a hospital.

Bolam came to a halt at the corner of the small cemetery next to a pile of rubble and bits of broken tree. A well-worn muddy path continued for around fifty yards to the buildings and tents. He'd start here, he thought as he swung his bag off his shoulder and sat down, perching carefully on a large stone. He fished out one of the books of paper and some charcoal. He hadn't used this medium at school but having fiddled with it over the past week, had found it quite forgiving. There were no complex shapes here. Only crosses, a dark dyke and the trees. This was ideal to start with and fitted perfectly with his plan only to draw simple things; no humans or animals, nothing with detail. He'd decided to avoid colour. Only black and white. He'd seen what had been called abstract art in a gallery in Newcastle once and didn't understand it, but here, for his purposes, he could see that by sticking to the basics, he might just get away with it.

After twenty minutes of sketching, Bolam was feeling quite pleased with himself. The shapes on his paper were coming together, white crosses contrasting with black skeletal shapes towering over them. "That looks interesting, son." The drawling voice cut into his concentration and startled Bolam, almost making him jump. A man stood behind him, peering over Bolam's shoulder. Nervously, Bolam raised himself to his feet and seeing the man's shirt and tie, could tell he was an officer. He clumsily tucked his drawing and charcoal under his arm and saluted. "You can relax, son." The officer's accent wasn't English and Bolam strained to see his uniform buttons for a clue. "This is a medical station, we're a bit less formal here. Major McCrae. I'm the surgeon here."

Bolam relaxed a little, "Lieutenant… Murray sir." He caught himself before the words came out; he'd need to get used to his identity if he was going to survive this.

"Murray. A Scotsman then? I thought you had a bit of an accent." It wasn't the first time Bolam had been mistaken for a Scot. He'd been assumed to be Liverpudlian, Welsh and Irish over the last six months or so.

"No, sir. From Newcastle, sir."

"Not that far off though. My family were Scots before they jumped on the boat to Canada."

"I couldn't place your accent either, sir. I was wondering, what with you not having your cap on."

"Field Artillery, but I work on men, not guns. Those over there, the ones below those crosses, some are the ones I couldn't save. Buried some myself…" The officer's eyes darkened. "Even friends." Bolam didn't know what to say, so simply nodded his understanding.

"You've captured it well. You know, the scene. Is it a hobby of yours?"

"It used to be, sir." Bolam knew this was the time to be sharp with his story. He'd rehearsed all manner of answers in his head for times like this. "I'm an official artist sir. I draw the war."

"I've heard of this. What do you do with the pictures then?"

"It depends, sir. Sometimes it's for headquarters, sometimes I send them to newspapers and magazines... that is, if they are allowed to be published."

"Ah. Had any luck? I've just sent something off to one myself."

"Not yet, sir." Bolam thought it was better to be unsuccessful as no one could then attempt to find his non-existing work. "But I live in hope." He smiled. "I wish you luck though."

The conversation was interrupted by a clattering of horses' hooves and a cart surged past the two men. "Wounded men coming in, sir." Another Canadian accent bellowed from the buildings.

"Murray, you want to see war? Come with me. I'll give you something to draw," McCrae said.

# 13<sup>th</sup> June, 1915, Ploegsteert

So far Bolam had visited seven medical installations of various types, but was avoiding the field hospital he'd been in when he was wounded. He'd hoped to make progress before having to return there, because the risk of discovery was so high. Over the past two weeks he'd spent time in dressing stations, casualty clearing stations and hospitals, and while none had shed any light on his case, all had opened his eyes. None more so than the two days he spent with Major McCrae in what he now knew was an advanced dressing station, taking the majority of the wounded coming in. Bolam had only witnessed some of those casualties arriving and being treated, but it was enough, and he could imagine what it must have been like in the thick of the battle that had raged for the previous two months.

He'd followed the surgeon that day, as he rushed to the aid of two soldiers brought in on the cart that had rattled past the pair as they'd discussed a strange mix of art, war and nationality. Bolam had watched as each man was rapidly assessed and the first, the one most likely to survive, whisked into the dimly lit operating theatre. The man had been hit directly in the kneecap by heavy machine gun fire and his leg hung on, attached only by tattered flesh and ligaments. He'd been given immediate first aid by the stretcher-bearer, who, despite his misgivings, Bolam watched closely for any signs that he may be his quarry. But none materialised.

Watching from just inside the doorway of the room, Bolam witnessed something more akin to the butcher's shop he's grown up near in Seaham. Blood and more blood. McCrae worked quickly and skilfully, carefully peeling back the tattered skin, sawing through bone (a sight Bolam had to turn away from) before trimming and sewing the skin back over the newly formed stump. The lower leg was taken away wrapped in a cloth to be incinerated later.

Throughout the next two days he witnessed five such operations, the last being the most distressing as the injury was to the soldier's face, and it was clear that if the man survived, his life would be very difficult indeed as so little was left of his lower jaw. Again, McCrae and his team worked tirelessly and with precision, despite the conditions, and managed to patch the man up in a state to be transferred to the next level of hospitalisation.

"So are you going to draw that for the generals, Murray?" McCrae had asked.

Bolam's expression conveyed the answer McCrae had expected.

Bolam did draw though. He needed to do so to preserve his cover story. He drew the shapes of the operating theatre; silhouettes of the scene, the instruments and patterns representing the blood. He knew they were fake and would be useless if he was ever challenged, but somehow, probably due to the intense conditions these people worked under, he was never questioned further. At night he walked back to 'his' cellar, having picked up some food from the stores at the dressing station.

There he pondered what he'd seen. There'd been plenty of opportunity for theft. Uniforms were cut off and discarded. But he was looking for a man who didn't collect from what was freely available. Bolam had watched all carefully. Stretcher-bearers, technicians and orderlies; all purposeful, all seemingly genuinely concerned to save lives, not to extinguish them. He began to doubt his theory; maybe this was the wrong line of enquiry? Maybe it was just too intense an environment to find a killer stalking the living?

By the end of the second evening, he had no answers to those questions, but his original theory still stood. These were men who had the autonomy to move around and he had to continue looking. If he'd been in Durham, if he hadn't seen the things he'd seen, he'd just keep focused on his line of enquiry until it led him one direction or another.

Three further dressing stations later, he'd kept to his story and found a way to watch and learn. Remarkably, no one questioned him too much. Many were interested in his drawings, even though he personally thought they were not worth the paper they were drawn on. Words like 'interesting' and 'unusual' were used to describe them, which Bolam privately took to mean that they weren't very good and even though he agreed, he felt slightly hurt.

Something else Bolam found remarkable here, were the people. All he'd come across were intensely passionate about their roles in this terrible situation. He'd studied all he'd met carefully. He'd witnessed how they'd looked at objects, people and their possessions. No one stood out. So here he was, back in the place where his plan had been born and also the most dangerous place for him to be at this point, with the exception of being back on the front line.

The ploy of just sitting drawing something had worked everywhere else, so he casually walked into the Ploegsteert field hospital and began drawing the scene. The shapes of the huts, tents and again, the trees behind them. There was something about trees; he had seen them in all the places he'd visited, all in different states of destruction and survival. This place was different though, they had leaves. They had suffered to a lesser extent and were growing. The others seemed devoid of life, almost as if they were looming over the wounded, sucking life force of others away to feed their own dwindling supply.

This place was much larger, even from his memories as a patient. It had grown and had almost become a small village, with a life of its own. There were more people here, more nurses; there'd been few of those at the dressing stations and it was a nurse who first spoke to him. Unlike his meeting with John McCrae, there was no confusion here.

He recognised the voice and inwardly panicked. "Excuse me, what are you doing here?" The voice sang as it had the first time he'd heard it, when he woke up in one of the nearby tents. The pretty Welsh nurse had never returned to Bolam's tent and he'd assumed she'd either been transferred or had taken up other duties. He'd hoped to see her again, remembering the kind way she spoke and the reassuring calmness in her voice. Instead, he'd spent too much time with a grumpy matron. Now, her voice that had calmed him that night terrified him. Beads of sweat formed instantly on his back and he felt his scalp begin to itch as its pores opened. If she recognised him…

Without turning to look at her, he answered her question, making every effort to suppress his northern accent. "I'm trying to capture the shapes of the tents and how they contrast with the organic nature of the trees." He couldn't believe he'd said that. Did it make sense? He'd never said anything like that before. It sounded so pretentious. But he kept on drawing and kept on facing away from his observer.

"I see. That's interesting." Bolam almost laughed. Bloody interesting, who'd have guessed? "We had an artist here once," she continued. Bolam shivered and his pores continued to weep. "Famous apparently. Even Winston Churchill came to see him…" She paused. "The day before he died."

Bolam worked hard to hold himself together. Not only had he stolen a man's property, and part of his identity, but it was now a dead man's life he had taken on. What could he say? He knew that there had to be a response and although he wanted to avoid conversation at all cost, he had to reply. "I'm so sorry to hear that. What was his name?"

For several minutes the nurse explained the name and all she knew about Muir. Bolam listened, continuously thinking how he could find a way to reply or to steer the conversation in another direction or indeed escape from the very nurse he'd once hoped to see again. Not now though. He wanted her to go, and quickly. Thankfully he was saved. Saved by the least likely angel. Matron. She called across to the nurse, speaking as gruffly to her as she'd done to him.

"I've got to go," the nurse said hurriedly and left.

Bolam sighed with relief and removed his cap. "Thank God for that," he said out loud.

126

"We do indeed have a lot to thank God for." Bolam's rapidly cooling scalp reheated instantly, as the confident voice of Reverend Edward Thompstone responded.

# 13<sup>th</sup> June, 1915, Ploegsteert

It was at that moment Bolam knew he'd made a grave mistake. He'd taken a calculated risk that no one would recognise him at the field hospital; after all, how many wounded soldiers would they see over a few months? He'd banked on the fact that he was one of hundreds of casualties passing through and on top of that he'd added his disguise. What he'd totally forgotten was that he'd seen Edward, his friend, at the hospital. It had been a brief encounter then he was gone and why his friend had disappeared and not returned had remained a reoccurring puzzle in Bolam's mind.

In the darkness of the night, when the guns roared and disturbed his sleep, Bolam had pondered this question many times. Had Edward been killed? He knew many of the chaplains took great risks, even entering the field of battle to comfort dying men. Had his friend done the same and succumbed?

The answer now stood directly behind him and Bolam froze. Not even the Germans had created this sort of panic within him. Yes, he'd been scared, terrified, but he drove himself on. This was different and he wasn't sure why.

"I didn't have you down for an artistic man, Frank."

The words shattered Bolam's spirit even more. So it was over. The game was up. There was no getting out of this now. His head dropped.

"I think we need to talk, don't you, Frank?" In the distance artillery rumbled, but Bolam hardly noticed. He was under fire in a very different way.

Three hours and five miles later Bolam sat in a dugout face to face with his friend. After a brief exchange, they'd walked the whole way almost in silence. Bolam didn't know what to say. He knew his investigation had failed and the likely next step was a court martial then the firing squad. He could be charged with a whole range of offences, from impersonating an officer to deserting his post. It wasn't death that he feared; he'd faced death before.

His pain burned because he'd failed to keep his promise. The promise he'd made to find the cold-blooded killer who had destroyed the lives of the living as well as his immediate victims. He pictured Mrs Bell, a broken woman left without income and with a child to bring up. He'd failed her. He'd failed them all. He remembered his old boss's words as he told him to put his investigation to one side, to end his 'fanciful theories'. How Charlton would scoff now after Bolam had ignored his advice only to end up a criminal himself.

The irony almost made him laugh. His friend caught the glimmer of a smirk as that thought flashed across Bolam's face.

"A smile Frank?" he said gently. "Want to share the joke?"

Bolam looked up. He'd discarded the glasses now. There was no reason to keep up the pretence now. "I'm not sure where to start, Edward." His voice faltered. "I think you're best not knowing. I don't want you involved."

"But I am involved, Frank. It's my job." He paused. "More than that, it's my duty as a friend. I have no idea what you've got into but I can help you."

A wry smile now emerged on Bolam's face and he chuckled. "Not this time. I don't think even God can fix this mess."

"Maybe you're right, Frank, but just for old times' sake let's talk about it. If you're right, you have nothing to lose."

Bolam had to admit he was right. He was going to die tied to a post, so what could be worse than that?

For the next forty minutes Bolam spoke and Edward listened, hardly interrupting, except to clarify a fact here and there. Bolam took his friend back to Durham, the murders, his initial cluelessness, his theory and his instructions to drop the case. This time he couldn't hold back and the irony of his situation caused him to erupt into short-lived laughter, slightly puzzling his friend who had been listening with great concentration.

Bolam talked Edward through every aspect of his plan to find the culprit; from its inception to the futility of his quest as he became engaged in the war and the events at the crater. It was at that point Bolam broke from his tale.

"So where did you go, Edward? You appeared in the tent when I was wounded and disappeared without a word."

Only a deafening silence came in reply to his question. In the dugout they were sheltered from all manner of evils, but not their thoughts. Bolam needed an answer and broke the stalemate.

"So, Edward, tell me. In your own words, what have you got to lose? I'm a dead man anyway. Where did you go?"

"Frank, let's just get through your story then I'll tell you. I want to help you, but I can't if you get side-tracked."

Bolam, exhausted with nervous tension, sighed. Back home he'd be like a dog at a bone and not waver from his line of enquiry. No, his energy was sapped and his will to win seemed burnt out. "Give me a moment," he agreed. "Then I'll continue."

He gained his composure, resumed his story and after a further half hour he led the reverend to the current point in time. His friend could not hide his discomfort and amazement at times. It did indeed sound improbable as Bolam retold his story. Indeed, who would spot a killer in this madness? Not me, he thought to himself. Not me.

# 14<sup>th</sup> June, 1915, Ypres

Bolam woke in almost total darkness. He was lying on his back on the rough sawn timber bed he'd sat on whilst talking to his friend the night before. Totally worn out, he hadn't argued when Edward suggested he got some sleep.

A candle flickered in the back of the dugout. He had no idea what time it was and carefully rolled off the straw mattress and felt his way slowly to the candle. His watch had stopped at 3.40 a.m. He knew he'd arrived at the dugout on the southern outskirts of Ypres in the late afternoon. Edward had explained that he'd been based here for several months and made his dutiful visits mostly by foot, supported by his batman. Bolam was yet to meet this man, but hoped he didn't have to. In fact, he wasn't sure he wanted to see anyone.

He guessed it was still dark outside but took the decision not to look. There was no way he'd have slept into the next day. His patterns of sleep were in tune with the battlefields and he'd become accustomed to only a few hours' sleep at a time. Even away from the front line he woke in a regular pattern through the night.

He turned his mind to the events of the previous day. He cursed. How stupid of him. He'd totally forgotten about Edward being in Belgium, even though he'd constantly worried about him!

Edward. Where was he now? Had he gone to report what Bolam had told him to the military police? He hadn't mentioned anything. In fact his friend had hardly said a word, let alone suggested any action. Edward had left him alone in the dugout. Left him alone again! What was his friend doing? Surely if he wanted to, he could escape from the dugout. Not that he had the energy or the desire. No, he'd come to the end. He knew his fate and as he stared back at the tiny stub of the candle, he simply felt numb.

Bolam had no idea how long his gaze had been fixed on the candle's mesmerising flame when the first dust plume fell from the ceiling. The floor shook and the earth around shuddered due to the explosion that had just occurred. Bolam was thrown to the ground. It seemed like the whole floor was rising and falling. He crawled to the bed and squeezed under it expecting the bombardment to carry on but nothing came. The earth stayed calm and silence fell.

Amazingly the candle in its wide based holder still flickered in the dust-filled space. The room seemed intact and thankfully the ceiling had held. Bolam knew it couldn't have been a direct hit, but it certainly must have been a powerful explosion to have rocked the dugout so dramatically. In the dim light, he looked around for any damage. There seemed to be little. Plenty of dirt and dust had been thrown but he could see no immediate danger from the structure of the place.

He reached out in the dark to drag himself out from his cover, pulling on an edge he felt near the boarded wall at the top end of the bed. Instead of him finding purchase, the edge came away and whatever he had grabbed fell away from the wall. Bolam tried again and this time wriggled free, using the edge of the bed for leverage. He crawled on hands and knees to the candle and sat with his back against the wall of the dugout. The candle flickered above his head and as the dust settled further he saw what had come away in his hands. A plank had come away from the wall where he had assumed it had been nailed. Despite his predicament he reached up, grabbed the candle and moved closer, intending to simply push the plank back into place.

Lowering his body to the floor he placed the candle to his side and reached out for the plank then stopped. Something glinted in the darkness in a recess where the plank had once sat. Moving the candle close solved the mystery. It was a bag. The brass catches on its side had reflected the light.

Bolam reached out and managed to grasp the handle of the bag. With his left hand he raised the plank to give himself more room. More dust flew upwards and he coughed as it caught in his throat. The bag was heavier than he expected but he managed to pull it free easily and slid it towards himself. A further effort brought the bag out from its hiding place and he sat up, staring at his find. A doctor's bag. Not unlike the one he'd stolen from the artist. Curiosity took over. Bolam's didn't consider whose bag it might be or why it might be there. A reflex action kicked in and he reached out and flipped the catches free.

The bag opened easily as Bolam raised the candle to examine the contents. He stared, open-mouthed. Instead of the medical supplies and instruments he might have expected to see, if indeed he had thought about what he might find inside, the bag shimmered and shone with buttons, insignia, medals and several crucifixes of differing designs and sizes. He recovered his composure and pulled the bag closer, gently extending the opening with both hands. Layers of items sat securely and neatly displayed. Someone had spent a lot of time creating this collection. This collection.

Bolam's brain shouted at him. The shock and enormity of the discovery hit him. There was no other explanation. His theory was right. He had been hunting a magpie after all and here was the proof.

Of all places, in his darkest hour, he'd found what he'd been looking for.

For the second time his brain screamed. Yes, he had his find, but of all the places... It was Edward's dugout that had revealed what he sought.

# 14<sup>th</sup> June, 1915, Ypres

Bolam sat in silence. Still shocked.

Everything had changed in the last five minutes. His best friend from Durham, a man of God for Christ's sake, the man he trusted more than any other, was now his prime suspect. Had Edward suspected the reason he'd enlisted when they met in the tent while injured? Is that why he'd disappeared? His mind swirled as he weighed it all up. Edward had brought him to this dugout. Why? He could have handed him over to the authorities back in Ploegsteert. Instead he'd brought him all the way to this place, kept him out of the way of others. 'For your safety, Frank.' Down in this darkness. It seemed now that it was more for Edward's safety than his!

It dawned on Bolam. Edward wasn't going to let him leave this place alive. It was clear now. He could blame Bolam. After all Bolam was a deserter. Who would blame the chaplain for defending himself against a madman disguised as an artist and with a false identity? He was cornered. He needed to get out of the dugout.

Bolam rose. His bag, the artist's bag, was in an alcove just outside the room. His gun was in there alongside his other possessions. He'd collect it on the way out. He'd just walk away. Walk out of the dugout and head for the nearest military policeman. Bolam placed his hand on the sackcloth curtain that acted as a door and made ready to leave. "Just grab your bag and move quickly, son," he said under his breath.

Bag! He needed the bag. It was his proof. Quickly he turned back and bent down, rushing to close the bag.

"Going somewhere, Frank?" The voice of Reverend Edward Thompstone shocked Bolam for the second time in two days.

Bolam recovered his composure quickly. "Actually, yes, Edward. I am. And I'm taking this bag with me."

"I'm not sure that's a good idea, Frank. That explosion you must have felt was a massive mine up at Hooge. There may well be more but Jerry will be pretty twitchy in any case. There's no point in putting yourself at risk."

"Putting myself at risk?" Bolam shouted. "Don't you think I've been doing that for the last few months? I don't think I'm any more at risk out there. Do you?" Bolam finished closing the bag, snapped the catches shut and stood up. "Edward, I'm going through that door. Don't try to stop me."

Before the reverend could reply, a hand drew the curtain back and a soldier stepped in.

"Are you all right, sir? I heard shouting." Bolam stared at the soldier. It was a face he'd never forget. Still hardened and still capped with straw coloured hair. Older without a doubt. Weathered somewhat. The man was much taller than when he'd last seen him, but he'd been a boy then.

"Arnold Wilson," Bolam breathed. "What on earth are you doing here?"

The man looked back at him without emotion. "I might ask y' the same question, Mr Bolam. Or should I call y' sir?"

"I don't mind what you call me right now, Arnold," Bolam said. At last he'd found an ally. "I need you to put Reverend Thompstone under arrest."

"You what, Frank?" The reverend's voice rose for the first time. "I don't think so. Have you gone raving mad? I knew you were capable of daft things, Frank, but arresting me?" He turned to leave and found a gun pointed straight at his stomach.

"Y' revolver I believe, Mr Bolam. Found it in that bag out there. Along, with some other interesting stuff. I wouldn't move quickly if were you, Reverend Thompstone. Nor you, sir. Both of y', sit down." Wilson jabbed the revolver forward indicating the floor.

Bolam and his friend looked at each other and slowly sat on the floor.

"Good. Now slide that bag forward to me."

Bolam looked up at the man. The boy's face was still there hidden by age and war, but it was still there. "You?"

Wilson looked back at him. His eyes were grey and cold. Bolam could see no compassion, no humanity in the man's eyes. Something else lived there, something broken and wrong.

"Are you surprised, Mr Bolam, sir?" He paused. "Oh, you thought it was him, didn't you? You had just collared your chum for a crime had you? Well, sorry to disappoint you."

The seated men looked at each other and Bolam's eyes dipped away from those of his friend.

"Frank?"

Bolam's silence gave his friend the answer he required. Edward looked up at his batman. "Wilson, what are you thinking? What do you think you are doing?"

"What do I think I'm doing, sir? Carrying on of course? Isn't that what we do, us privates? Carry on. I don't know how many times you or some other officer said that to me. Well, that's what I'm doing. That's what I have been doing since I came to this godforsaken place after he" – he jabbed the revolver again, but this time at Bolam – "wouldn't stop looking. He just wouldn't give up. And now the bastard is here."

"Arnold. I looked after you. I got you away from your troubles." Bolam stared at the man. Maybe there was still something of the boy left there.

Wilson smirked. "Troubles. What would you know? A bloody policeman. You got me out all right, but what for? My nightmares never stopped. Those bloody do-gooders at the cathedral. One of them wouldn't leave me alone. Always there, following me. Interested in me he said. He was interested in me all right but not the sort of interest I wanted. I'd had enough of grown men abusing me.

"He tried it on time after time and one day he thought he'd corner me after the other masons had gone home. Not always the best plan to pick on someone with a hammer in their hand eh?" He paused and smiled. "Anyway, he's still at the cathedral, or under it if you get my meaning. The dirty sod is now a foundation stone."

He laughed out loud. "He was my first and my inspiration." He reached into his pocket and pulled out a chain which stretched out, obviously held inside by a pin or clasp of some kind. At the end was a button. "See this? This small button was the start of my collection. It's

139

nothing special, but it's my memento, my reminder that I will never be controlled or dominated again."

Bolam looked back, his heart sank; it could have been anyone but no it had to be the boy he'd saved. He'd tried to do good but it had backfired. Would this young man be a killer if he'd been ignored by Bolam all those years ago? Bolam's mind spun with confusion and shock and his head hung low. He was tired. The search had taken its toll and he wanted it to be over. But not this way.

A low laugh, almost a mocking chuckle woke Bolam from his stupor. Looking up he could see Wilson smirking and twitching the barrel of the revolver from side to side, almost as if he was choosing where to shoot Bolam. Bolam raised his head fully and looked back into Wilson's eyes and smiled, now realising the truth. "It's more than just a memento isn't it, Arnold? It's not about collecting objects is it? You collect the kills. You enjoy killing."

Wilson quickened the gun's movement, swinging it even further. "Once again, Mr Bolam, you are right, sir."

The gunshot in the small room was deafening. It seemed that the air had exploded around them and Bolam ducked automatically and rolled over onto the floor. His ears rang with the echo of the shot but he felt nothing. No pain. To his right Reverend Thompstone lay in a similar position. A short cough erupted from him and his body shuddered. Bolam pushed himself up onto his knees and bent over his friend, thinking he'd been concussed from the noise. A dribble of blood ran from the reverend's mouth and dripped to the dusty floor.

Bolam used all his strength to try to turn his friend who spluttered again. Something wet seeped into Bolam's fingers and looking down he saw a blood stain. He'd seen such things many times on the battlefield. Wilson had shot

Edward. He looked up at the killer. A tiny beam of light sneaked through the edge of the curtain and slashed across Wilson's face. He was smiling.

"Why?" said Bolam.

"It was only a matter of time and now seems to be as good as any. I was at his every beck and call. Back in harness again. Besides, I always liked his cap badge!"

Bolam threw himself at Wilson, surging up from the floor, using his momentum to power into his torso and to knock his gun hand away. The gun fired and another shot blasted the room. This time it was no surprise and Bolam was not shaken. He held his nerve and drove on. He was on top of Wilson now, grappling with the man. Bolam swung with his left arm aiming a punch at the man's face but caught Wilson's shoulder with his elbow, drilling into it. Wilson screamed, dropped the gun and writhed on the ground, trying to free himself, but Bolam pressed on, consumed by anger and the long suppressed hatred for this killer.

By now they'd fallen through the curtain and into a small low tunnel. Light shone in from the outside and seemed to spur Wilson on as he burst free, fleeing the maddened Bolam and dashing toward the light. Bolam pursued quickly, desperately trying to gain ground.

It was only a short tunnel, dark and slippery under foot. Ahead, he saw Wilson a few yards ahead of him struggling to maintain balance. Bolam launched himself at the man, pushing his feet into the mud and thrusting forward. As the tunnel turned it opened directly onto a trench and the change from dark to bright sunlight temporarily blinded Wilson who paused instinctively and threw his hands to his eyes. Bolam, a second behind him, crashed into the static man.

Both fell forward onto the putrid mud of the trench floor, each man immediately reacting; Wilson attempting to push away, Bolam straining to hold the man down. Several Tommies further down the trench were startled into battle readiness as if the Germans had invaded their trench but relaxed slightly when they could see it was two of their own. Nevertheless, several of them advanced quickly, one screaming, "There's snipers out there, get a grip on yourselves."

At that moment, Wilson struggled free and, twisting on to his back, lashed his right foot into Bolam's face, instantly breaking his nose and splitting his upper lip. Blood filled Bolam's mouth and gushed from his nostrils, but the adrenalin pushed him on. Shaking his head he knelt up and scrambled after the fleeing Wilson.

The Tommy screamed another warning but it fell on deaf ears and both men continued their desperate struggle along the trench. Bolam rose to his feet seconds behind Wilson who he could see was now beginning to run having gained his footing. Bolam forced himself forward but his progress was immediately halted. A strong arm grabbed him around the waist as he began to stand and dragged him backwards. He looked on as Wilson made his escape glancing back at him with a smirk as he saw Bolam now being held low by a soldier.

As Bolam looked on, screaming for the soldier to release him, the right side of Wilson's smug head exploded into pink mist that flooded the air as bone and brain decorated the mud of the trench. Limply, Wilson's legs buckled and he dropped to his knees folding into the trench wall, his face crashing into the mud.

Bolam watched as the boy he'd helped many years ago slowly slid lifeless down the side of the trench and slumped face first into the slime of the trench floor. "Don't move!" a voice screamed and Bolam looked up to find three Lee Enfield rifles pointed straight at him.

# 19<sup>th</sup> June, 1915, Poperinge

The town hall in Poperinge stood tall looking over the main square. Below its neo-gothic spires all manner of people passed south through its shadow bringing war and its instruments to the area. Arriving in the town from the south was usually a different affair; men on leave came for relaxation and relief from the front line. However, under the building, away from the *estaminets*, clubs and hustle and bustle above, the town jail catered for a different clientele. And on this day Bolam was the sole occupant.

Five days had passed since the events in the dugout. Bolam's life, as if it had not been difficult then, had suddenly taken a turn for the worse, and worse still exponentially. Today was to be his last. The fate he'd accepted on meeting Edward again was to come to fruition. Tomorrow he'd leave this room and walk to the wall near the church. His hands would be bound, but they'd be re-tied, this time around a wooden post. He'd be blindfolded and several men would stand in front of him. It could be twelve men, maybe as few as six. He'd never know as he wouldn't hear the shots as the command came and they pulled the triggers on their rifles. The same type of rifles that had been pointed at his head outside the dugout. The memory of those events would remain burned into his memory until the first bullet struck his heart.

Back outside the dugout Bolam had raised his hands immediately, not moving. However, he didn't stay quiet. "I need to go back in, your chaplain is in there and he's wounded," he said, carefully looking into the eyes of each of the men pointing their weapon at him. His head stayed perfectly still, only his eyes moved. He didn't want to provoke any twitch of a finger on a trigger. The men looked at each other and back to Bolam. "I need to go back in," he insisted. "That man has just shot your chaplain." Again the men exchanged glances, but this time he could see they were uncertain. He took the risk. He was a dead man anyway. "I will move now. I will make no sudden moves. Follow me in and you will see." Again he caught all eyes with his, and then he moved.

No shots came. He turned slowly, keeping his hands raised before stooping to duck into the tunnel. The men followed, rifles still pointing at Bolam.

In the dugout, Bolam found his friend as he'd left him. Blood still ran from his mouth and Bolam could see from the splatters he'd continued coughing. Bolam carefully pulled back his jacket. The bullet had entered his stomach.

"Get me a first aid kit," he ordered, turning back towards the first of the three men behind him. "Quickly!"

A small hessian bag was soon passed to him and he speedily fished out and opened a gauze pad, pressing it onto his friend's wound. "Edward. Edward, can you hear me?" he said. A flicker of eyes and a slight movement of his friend's head suggested some recognition. "I'm going to get you to help, Edward. Open your eyes."

Slowly, Reverend Edward Thompstone opened his eyes. He coughed again and more blood splattered. Pain creased his face, then he smiled. His eyes opened wider and he smiled again and nodded, staring directly at Bolam, who now realised there was no hope. He'd seen this sort of wound before and knew neither he nor a surgeon like John McCrae could save his friend. He'd die before they got him out of the trench.

"Edward. I'm sorry," he said. "I didn't expect any of this. I didn't mean…" His words were cut short. In what must have been a Herculean effort, his friend moved his hand and touched Bolam's mouth. His eyes once again widened and his head moved gently from side to side. With one last piercing look his eyes closed for the last time. Bolam sank, placed his head on his friend's chest and sobbed.

Between Bolam and the three men they carried Edward's body from the dugout and summoned a stretcher-bearer. Fifteen minutes later, Bolam watched as the only real friend he'd had at home was placed on a stretcher, covered with a tarpaulin and strapped down before being carried along the trench and back towards the town. It seemed like only days since they had been sitting in Bolam's living room, drinking, laughing, discussing fishing. He could not have imagined this in his wildest dreams.

It took Bolam several minutes before he composed himself. He knew what he must do now. After gathering both his bag and Wilson's, he returned to the trench and spoke to the soldiers gathered there. "What you have witnessed is the result of greed and murder. Good men die here every day, but Private Wilson here…" He paused and looked toward the slumped body still prone in the mud, causing all who'd gathered to follow his gaze. "Private Wilson was a devious murderer who joyfully took lives in

146

England and here. I intend to walk to headquarters and report this. You are welcome to take me there, to arrest me, if you feel I am guilty, but either way, the truth needs to be told."

One of the soldiers, a sergeant who'd pointed his rifle at Bolam earlier spoke. "Sir, I will come with you, but not with a rifle at your back. I can see this was not your doing. You'll need some help with those bags and maybe some help explaining this."

Bolam nodded and a wry smile crept over his face. "Indeed I will, Sergeant, indeed I will."

It was a slow and silent walk to headquarters some two miles away. Chateau Rosendal, or Bedford House as it was known to the British Tommies, had once been a grand chateau with a moat and carefully manicured gardens. The British had made it area HQ once they had taken over from the French and consequently the German artillery had made many efforts to shell the building. The once grand building was shattered and pock marked with the pounding it had taken, but still, its cellars and intact buildings remained and served their new masters.

Bolam arrived with his escort. The way into the grounds of Bedford House was churned with mud; months of horses, carts and wagons had turned any discernible road into what seemed like a sludge filled river. Along with others arriving and leaving, the two men picked their way along the edge, being careful not to lose their balance as falling one way into the mud would be lethal and the deep moat that still remained on the other side seemed just as uninviting.

A guard of two men stood to attention by what remained of a doorway in what remained of a corner of the building. Bolam approached, placed Wilson's bag on the floor, saluted and addressed one of the men. "Private, I need to speak to your commanding officer."

Quite clearly these men had been given orders to deter anyone without specific orders. Bolam was unable to show any on request and the more frustrated Bolam became, the more the men seemed immovable until an officer appeared behind them. "What is the commotion here? I thought you two had strict instructions."

"They clearly do, sir." Bolam saluted. The man held a much higher rank than he. His insignia suggested he was a major. "I've had no joy from them. I urgently need to report a problem, sir."

The major looked Bolam up and down, glanced at the sergeant and said stiffly, "Very well, follow me."

"Do you have any military police here, sir?" Bolam interjected before he moved. "We'll be needing their help too, sir."

The major nodded at one of the guards. "Black, see if you can find one of the Redcaps." Then he turned to Bolam. "Will that be everything? We haven't got all day you know."

Bolam sighed inwardly. This wasn't going well. Just what he needed, a stuffy fart of an officer. He remembered his mother's words… *Don't think you'll get respect, son.* He retrieved the artist's bag from the sergeant, picked up his bag of evidence and followed the officer.

Inside the door was a narrow staircase leading up to a shattered landing. Bolam could see the sky through the remains of the ceiling above it and tatters of curtains swayed gently around the broken window looking down at him. The once decorative walls echoed their past with what was left of painted borders and mouldings. To the left was another staircase, this time heading down. "Close the door behind you, Lieutenant," the major said. Bolam did as he was asked and followed downward.

The air was musty and a faint tinge of alcohol snipped at Bolam's nostrils. Wine, he guessed. Or beer. After descending several yards, the stairs swung left and they emerged into a large dimly lit room. A large rough table sat under a single oil lamp. Two others hung centrally from the ceiling. He'd been right. The empty racks, no doubt drained by soldiers, had once housed a large wine store.

Voices came from his right and he was surprised to see two more men, both officers, appear from another door hidden in the shadows. Their voices seemed almost jovial, not at all as he had expected having met the major. He breathed a sigh of relief inwardly and once again stood to attention as they approached.

"Stand easy, Lieutenant." The taller of the two spoke, his accent clearly northern but like Bolam, he'd obviously either never picked up the full strength of the accent or had decided to lose it. Bolam guessed the former. Few men like him made the higher ranks. "Major, can you explain our guest's visit please?"

The major, as uneasy and stuffy with these officers as he was with Bolam, stumbled through an explanation. "Hopefully one of the Redcaps will join us, sir. Though I am not sure why."

"Well, Lieutenant?" The officer looked back at Bolam.

"It's a long story, sir, and not an easy one to tell."

It appeared Bolam was indeed in the company of a fellow northerner, though not from Durham. Lieutenant Colonel Powell invited Bolam to sit. This had never happened to Bolam in such company before and the raised eyebrows of the major suggested he didn't approve. The shorter officer, a fellow lieutenant, who accompanied Powell, listened without speaking for the whole of Bolam's time in the room.

Bolam began his explanation with what he realised later was a mistake. "Three hours ago a fellow officer, a chaplain, was murdered." By this time a military policeman had arrived, a sergeant, who, on hearing Bolam's first words took out a pencil and notebook.

For over an hour Bolam explained. He took the small gathering back to Durham, explained his reasons for enlisting, the fruitlessness of his initial time in Ypres and then his change of identity. Throughout, the major's face looked as if it was cast in stone except for the occasional frown. However, the words, *so I became Jameson Murray*, caused all present to sit upright and the standing Redcap to step forward.

There was a long pause before Powell spoke. "I suppose there's more? There had better be, Lieutenant. This isn't sounding very healthy for you."

"I realise that, sir," said Bolam, before carrying on to explain the events of the last few weeks, how a chance meeting and an improbable event became a false theory and how a ghost from his past developed into a spectre who'd haunted him for several years. Finally, he summed up the events of that morning. The death of his friend at the hands of that very spectre. He'd shown them the artist's bag and finally, towards the end, opened up Wilson's bag to reveal his grisly collection. There was a sharp intake of breath as layer upon layer of shining brass and silver gleamed on the table under the light of the oil lamp. Beautifully polished buttons and badges, medals, both British and German, even coins and cloth insignia, each one representing a life taken, all laid out carefully as if in a museum case. Bolam guessed there were over twenty lives contained in this one case. Was there another case like this back in Durham, he wondered?

When he finished, there was silence.

# 20th June, 1915, Poperinge

Bolam woke early. Not that he needed an alarm call. He was going to be shot and while he'd accepted his fate, he didn't relish it. Like most men, he'd harboured thoughts of a family, despite his age, and hoped some day to meet someone like the pretty Welsh nurse and settle down. Too late for that. He'd slept fitfully, drifting in and out of scenarios from the past months, playing them over and over in his mind. Some of them became warped dreams where the evils of the trenches became even more gruesome and destructive. In one, the German, Kaningasser, whose mother would now never hear of her son's death, rose up before him and walked back to his own lines only to be cut down by the machine guns of his comrades. But mostly he replayed the General Court Martial. The day he learned his life was to end against a post.

After his explanation at Bedford House, Bolam was arrested.

"I must admit I have never heard such a tale," Powell admitted. "I will leave it to the MPs to settle."

With that Bolam was handcuffed and marched out of the cellar under the guard of the Redcap sergeant. The next few days passed slowly but to Bolam they were blurred. He'd been moved twice, always under guard, always closely supervised by military policemen despite his assurances. "You know, Sergeant, I volunteered myself. I'm hardly going to make a run for it."

Clearly taught to not fraternise with his charges, the sergeant simply nodded.

The General Court Martial was held in Poperinge, above the cell he now waited in. The room itself was quite welcoming and smelled of old oak, though the mood of foreboding outshone it. Prior to the war, the daily business that graced the room was much more mundane, being mostly concerned with local politics and trade. The room now had a much more challenging role.

Despite the initial reluctance of the Redcaps to enter into conversation, over time, the tension had eased and it was apparent that there was as much unease amongst them about the possibility of a death sentence as there was with rank and file soldiers. The two who accompanied Bolam from his cell to the court martial had done their best to lighten Bolam's mood, with small talk about football and cricket back in England. One, it seemed, had been a promising sportsman and still held an ambition to play at the highest level in both sports. Nevertheless, for all their efforts, Bolam remained quietly restrained.

The formality of the affair was almost as unsettling as the charge levelled against him. Desertion was one of several charges that carried the death penalty. In fact Bolam could have been charged with a few of the others, but it seemed the fact that he'd admitted to leaving his post was the overriding charge to the prosecuting officers.

Bolam stood to attention when the three officers in charge of proceedings arrived and was not allowed to sit again even though his legs nearly buckled when he saw who had arrived in the room. He knew the charge against him was grave and that the likelihood was he would be found guilty. He'd expected the proceedings to be a mere formality but did not expect the humiliation of coming face to face with his old boss from Durham.

Lieutenant Colonel Charlton stared at Bolam with burning eyes and a look of contempt which shook the man on trial. It took all Bolam's willpower to avoid turning his face to the floor. He could feel Charlton's eyes burning into him, no doubt with a huge degree of dissatisfaction to see a man he had mentored as an officer of the law on trial for his life. Yet, somewhere inside him Bolam took a small shred of hope from the arrival of Charlton. At least, he hoped, Charlton had always been a fair man, and if nothing else, he would be listened to.

Of the group of three officers, Charlton came second in terms of rank. A full colonel led the panel that would decide Bolam's future. A captain Bolam had met on his arrival in Ypres made up the complement. Led by the colonel, the three officers, supported by two clerks and the Redcaps, followed army protocol to the letter. On request, Bolam, representing himself having declined an offer of support, carefully answered every question put to him and then explained his motives and reasoning in depth, using Wilson's bag as his evidence. He'd been over and over his story since his meeting at Bedford House, honing every aspect of his case to illustrate the justice of his case as well as possible. Still he held out no hope he'd be seen as anything more than a criminal in the eyes of British Army law. His greatest worry was that he had no access to his notes and the documents he put together in Durham. There was little he could do to illustrate thoroughly his thinking prior to enlisting.

Bolam called no witnesses but took a risk given the make up of the panel. "If I may, Colonel, I would like Lieutenant Colonel Charlton to testify regarding my character, my honesty and integrity…" This indeed was a risk, as there was every possibility that Charlton would not wish to taint his own career by association with such a criminal. "…if he would be predisposed to do so?"

There was some muted discussion among the panel before the decision. "Very well. It is most irregular but I will allow it," came the stuffy reply.

Surprisingly Charlton spoke both highly and passionately of Bolam as a police officer, but tempered his statement with a phrase that dampened Bolam's spirits. "But of course, I couldn't vouch for him now, nor for any of his motives for behaving in such a peculiar and clearly irrational manner."

The process took less than an hour and the three officers retired to make a decision. Throughout this recession Bolam continued to stand while the clerks and Redcaps chatted and became more agitated as time lingered on. He heard one clerk whisper, "I've never known it take this long." This caused a raised eyebrow from the other and turned the heads of both of his guards. Bolam had no idea what to make of this statement. Was it a good thing, or not?

It was over forty minutes later when the three returned and Bolam learned his fate. There was little ceremony, certainly no sentiment. His sentence was passed quickly and clinically without any explanation or justification, only that he had, 'Behaved in an extreme manner, contrary to the law of the British Army, betraying his fellow soldiers.' And as such the panel had no choice but to give the maximum sentence. As the final words of sentencing were uttered, Charlton avoided Bolam's eye, staring firmly at the desk in front of him.

After waking, Bolam didn't eat. He drank a mug of tea but refused food. Why bother? Time dragged until his cell door was opened and the Redcaps stood, brows furrowed, ready to take him to his death.

*\*\*\**

Those present at the burial of Frank James Bolam knew they'd buried a good man. They knew he'd fought bravely. They knew he'd served his country well, both in the army and in civilian life. They knew he'd loved his family and given so much to the community. Those who witnessed his death said that he'd left this earth smiling, looking at the sky. They said that he knew he'd had a good life and was lucky to have lived as long as he had. Not many folks survived the trenches and made it to the ripe old age of 101.

It wasn't until his son, Joseph, who had the unenviable task of sorting through his father's personal possessions, discovered the shoebox, that the truth about those days in the trenches came to light. Frank, like most veterans of that war, played his cards close to his chest, revealing very little of the horrors he'd experienced. Joe and the rest of the family knew that Frank had served in the war, and knew he'd fought bravely as he'd been awarded a medal. What they didn't expect was the story that the box revealed in a collection of letters and notebooks.

# Extract from the Notebook of Frank Bolam,
# Dated 23rd June 1915

Today I am on my way back to England. Two days ago I died in Poperinge, or at least a part of me did.

When the Redcaps came for me, I can only remember taking a long breath and forcing myself to straighten my legs to stand up away from the bench in my cell. I didn't want to be weak. It was bad enough being labelled a traitor to the country so I wanted to die well. What I didn't expect to see was Charlton, Lieutenant Colonel Charlton to give him his military title, my old boss, outside the door. He had a stern look about him and I guessed wrongly that he'd come to say something to me about him telling me not to carry on with the case. About how stupid I had been. And how I had let him down after what he'd done for me.

I could not have been more wrong.

Rather than being escorted outside and across the road to my death, the Redcaps left and I was ushered by Charlton up some stairs into a small room. He did indeed tell me I was stupid and he did indeed remind me what he'd said to me back in Durham, but he then surprised me by producing papers discharging me from the army with immediate effect. I have to say I nearly fainted. I'd been preparing for my imminent death and then I was being given a way out. I remember asking why they'd do such a thing.

Charlton told me that after the court martial hearing, when he and the other three officers met to decide my fate, he had persuaded the other two that there was an alternative way. None of them had disagreed that I had been a deserter. In fact, all agreed I should be shot. However, it seems that Charlton, having been a policeman, knew what had driven me to do what I did. He also knew that the people whose lives had been shattered by Wilson back in Durham needed some closure. So he and the others decided that Frank Bolam would not die and another would take his place.

# *Murders Solved by War Hero*

Four previously unsolved murders have been revealed to be the work of a soldier killed in Belgium, says the newly promoted Chief Superintendent Frank Bolam.

Having fought and been injured in Belgium, winning the Military Cross for bravery, Bolam explains that while out there he became suspicious after hearing some stories about a particular soldier. A German sniper killed Arnold Wilson, 19, of Durham, before Bolam could investigate further, but on arrival back in England, having been honourably discharged after injury, the Chief Superintendent picked up the case.

"When we searched Wilson's property, we found a hoard of artefacts relating to the murders," said Chief Superintendent Bolam.

The discovery gives some peace to the relatives of Wilson's victims. Edna Bell, 44, the wife of James Bell who was one of Wilson's victims said, "I am grateful to Mr Bolam. He told me he'd find the killer and he did. He's a good man, just like my James was."

# Extract from a Letter to Frank Bolam, Dated 21st February 1920

*Thank you for letting me know how my son died. I know he was a brave man.*

The letter was signed,

*Frau Kaningasser.*

# 26<sup>th</sup> July 1982, Lijssenthoek Military Cemetry, Poperinge

The morning mist clung to the grass, struggling to hang on as the sun cut through the trees. The rows of limestone headstones shone as they stood uniformly and neatly to attention, as those below them had done so well many years ago.

Joseph Bolam and his son, James, stood in front of two graves. Coincidentally placed together? Joe thought not. He'd read all of his father's notebooks so many times he had a feeling that this was not an accident. It was a strange feeling. He knew that both of these men in different ways had given his father, and subsequently himself and his son, their future. Neither father nor son spoke, they knew what to do and stooped, slowly and carefully together before each placing an inscribed wooden cross. One on each grave. They both paused, wet eyes blurring their vision, then stood. A final look, a glance and a nod at each other, then they turned and left, leaving the graves of Rev. E. Thompstone and Lt. J. Muir. Both crosses read simply, *Friend.*

# Historical Note

Sometime around 1965 my Nana showed me a book that was to have a huge impact on me. She referred to it as the 'War Book', although it was more than that. The book was a pictorial history of the first twenty-five years of the twentieth century and naturally contained a rich content of photographs from the Great War. I visited my Nana regularly as we lived only doors away from her house in the small mining village in which I grew up. This book inspired many questions about the time and events, and my Nana, who was aged only six at the onset of the war, did her best to answer them. She told me tales of heroism and sang songs from the time. From that point on I have had a fascination with World War One and particularly the events in France and Belgium. I still have the 'War Book' which remains a family heirloom.

While I've tried to be as accurate as possible with historical facts, even down to the type of bicycle Bolam used, I have made one or two alterations. In order to get Bolam out to Ypres quickly, I accelerated the pace of his training. Training for an officer would normally have taken around a year, but for the purposes of Bolam's task, he had a crash course on being an officer and was out there in a few months. Having said that, later on in the war recruits were indeed appearing in France after only a few weeks of training. It was also not likely at the time that Bolam could have become an officer, it was only later that those of lesser standing were accepted, but more often after already serving in the forces and showing leadership qualities. A great example of this was Walter Tull, who despite military law stating that a 'negro or person of colour' could not be in charge, was so highly thought of by his superiors that he was promoted to become the first black combat officer.

Officer training did indeed cover such things as machine gun tactics, although the British were in fact woefully behind the Germans in this area and did not effectively deploy them or realise the techniques of planes of fire to create killing zones until late in the war. General Haig was an opponent of the use of the machine gun (amongst other developments such as the helmet and airplane) thinking it might dampen the men's attacking spirit. Haig much preferred the use of 'horse and sabre', keeping tens of thousands of mounted troops ready for the breakthrough that would never come, and was responsible for the tactics aiming to give the breakthrough at the Somme.

At the time Bolam was joining up, the Pals battalions were forming; a strategy used to encourage enlistment through loyalty and peer pressure, a strategy that was to prove disastrous for both regiments and communities alike. Most of the Pals battalions spent the whole of 1915 training in readiness for the offensive we now know as The Battle of the Somme. For many it would be their first battle and also their last. Although our action takes place in Ypres, it is worth noting that on the first day of the Somme, 1st July 1916, the British army, including many Pals battalions, walked into a nightmare. 60,000 casualties, of which 20,000 were dead. Amongst these figures are the 584 members of the 720 Accrington Pals who were missing, wounded or dead. At the same time the Leeds Pals lost around all but 150 of the 900 strong battalion that went over the top. The effect of these weighty casualties meant that whole communities were devastated.

Wounds varied in seriousness and with new ways of killing and maiming they were sometimes complex. Medicine was also more sophisticated, so wounds that may well have killed a generation earlier were now treatable. When Bolam was in the field hospital, the term 'Blighty Wound' was used. Blighty was typically used affectionately by British troops to describe their home nation, popularised by poets such as Wilfred Owen and in songs of the time. A 'Blighty Wound' was an injury not serious enough to kill, but one that would require further treatment back in Britain. Oddly, other than the obvious causes such as gunshot wounds, it appears that frogs caused a significant number of injuries. The little amphibians loved the trenches and regularly caused men to slip and break a leg!

The Belgian town of Poperinge, or 'Pop' or even 'Pops' as it was known to the Tommies, played an interesting role at the time. While it was regularly bombed, it was generally known as a place of rest and recuperation for soldiers. An *estaminet* is a sort of pub and there were indeed *estaminets* of the sort Bolam visited, but also there was Toc H. Toc H became a place of sanctuary and rest for soldiers set up by the Reverend 'Tubby' Clayton. The place became an 'Everyman's club', as opposed to the Skindles Hotel not far away, which only catered for officers. Its name comes from the radio signallers' code for its initial letters. Later, in 1920, Clayton established Toc H as a Christian youth centre in London and then as an international charitable organisation.

Ploegsteert, or Plug Street, as the Tommies jokingly named it, is village near the French border which saw little action during the war. The dressing station situated there was nicknamed 'Charing Cross'. The Royal Army Medical Corps established an effective Chain of Evacuation to ensure the quick retrieval and treatment of injured soldiers. The Regimental Aid Posts, set just behind the front lines and field dressing stations, like Bolam's temporary accommodation, were all part of this. Apart from Bolam, Winston Churchill is known to have spent time in Belgium during his self-imposed exile to the trenches, although this was not as early as I have included him. Churchill did indeed spend time in Ploegsteert and like Bolam, made many forays into no man's land.

Ypres (or Wipers, as the Tommies knew it) itself has been rebuilt in a remarkable fashion. By the time Bolam arrived there was already significant destruction of the medieval buildings, and in particular the beautiful Cloth Hall. By 1918 there was hardly anything recognisable of the town at all. The fact that it has been restored to near its former glory and that the Cloth Hall is now the venue for the In Flanders Fields Museum, is testament to the hardships the people of the area had to suffer.

The small cemetery, where Bolam made his first sketch, was Essex Farm, now a pristine and well visited Commonwealth Cemetery. Right next to it are the remains of the concrete bunker-like buildings where Major John McCrae spent time as a surgeon, and at one point wrote the famous poem, 'In Flanders Fields', possibly inspired by the death of a good friend, Lieutenant Alexis Helmer. McCrea did actually 'bury' his friend, and in the absence of a chaplain, he apparently said the appropriate words. As a teacher, this little cemetery is possibly one of the most moving places I have taken students, not just because of the connection with John McCrae, but also because of the grave of one of the youngest to be killed on the western front, Rifleman Valentine Joe Strudwick, aged fifteen.

The youth of Rifleman Strudwick is shocking in the sense that we know his age. Thousands of underage boys joined up, still not even shaving, lying about their age. The most common age given was nineteen, as this was the age where you were eligible to be sent overseas to fight. So, for those readers who spotted the age change in Arnold Wilson; although sixteen when he joined up, he is reported to be nineteen in the newspaper article because of the likelihood he would have given this age as his own.

While in the dugout Bolam is caught in the shock wave from a huge explosion and later learns from his friend, Edward Thompstone, that it was the detonation of a massive amount of explosive in a mined tunnel at Hooge. At the time this was the largest explosion ever to have been made, although it happened on 19th July 1915, several days later than the time I had Bolam experience it. Like Essex Farm, for anyone visiting the area, this is worth a look and not only is there the remains of the crater, now flooded, there are trenches and pillboxes to explore.

The second Battle of Ypres ended on 25th May 1915 after just over a month of severe and bloody fighting. For Bolam, it was convenient as when the guns fell silent, it allowed him the space to travel in the area. However, as

Wilson found, hostilities did not end, there was still sporadic fighting, mining and of course snipers still happy to shoot, if you were daft enough to stick your head above the top of the trench.

The Second Battle of Ypres was a bloody affair and thousands of men lost their lives defending the town and surrounding area. The Germans brought gas to the war which took the Allies totally by surprise. There was little protection from the heavy clouds of green that billowed over and flooded into trenches, described by Lieutenant C. W. G. Ince as a, '… terrible stream of death'. Eyes burned and many died at their posts. Bolam's tactic of hiding up a tree was indeed employed by some soldiers as they had learned that the gas stayed low.

In my career as a teacher and head teacher, I have led many school trips abroad. Possibly the one I am most proud of is a development that came from the thinking of several like minds. In an attempt to create really meaningful cross curricular links, Chris Henley, the Head of Languages, Michyla Rossa, the second in the English Department, Kathryn Smith, Head of Humanities and I developed an extension to the school's existing 'Paris Trip'. Its combination of hands-on history and literacy teaching while in Ypres became a hugely successful part of the school's extra-curricular learning provision, eventually to become a separate trip. Some of the powerful learning experiences I have witnessed there will stay with me forever, but one stands out.

A student once asked me on a visit to the Menin Gate why the war was called a world war. It was easy to illustrate part of the answer by showing him the lists of the 55,000 lost soldiers on the walls of that fantastic monument, including those from New Zealand, Australia, Canada, India, China, Afghanistan, and so on.

He turned to me and said, "I am so proud that my family name is on this wall and they fought for Britain." His surname was Khan and he had managed to find his way by boat, foot and other means to Leicester, fleeing the Taliban in his home town in Afghanistan. It still moves me to write about it today, many years after the event.

There are so many true stories of heroism and hardship related to the First World War. Men of all backgrounds fought in the most appalling conditions in a new type of conflict where technology evolved to create killing at a new level. The armies of both sides struggled to adapt and men paid the price. Still, even in the depths of such darkness, humanity lived on and there are lots of examples of opposing sides having treated each other with empathy and respect. Hopefully through Bolam's trials and tribulations, some of the history of the era illustrates all of these things while giving Bolam the scope to solve a crime.